OBSOLETE
SPELLS

OBSOLETE SPELLS:

POEMS & PROSE FROM
VICTOR NEUBURG
& THE VINE PRESS

EDITED BY
JUSTIN HOPPER

Obsolete Spells: Poems & Prose from Victor Neuburg & The Vine Press
Edited by Justin Hopper

First published by Strange Attractor Press © 2022
Foreword © 2022 Richard McNeff
Introduction © 2022 Justin Hopper
Afterword © 2022 Margaret Jennings-White

Set in 10pt Jenson Pro
Layout/Design by Maïa Gaffney-Hyde

ISBN: 9781913689261

Strange Attractor Press
BM SAP, London,
WC1N 3XX, UK
www.strangeattractor.co.uk

Distributed by The MIT Press, Cambridge, Massachusetts.
And London, England.

Printed and bound in Estonia by Tallinna Raamatutrükikoda.

'Sir, you have wrestled well, and overthrown
more than your enemies.'

LIST OF ILLUSTRATIONS

TABLE OF CONTENTS

TABLE OF CONTENTS

FOREWORD

BY RICHARD MCNEFF

The more time you spend with Victor Neuburg, the more you come to like him. With his 'thin venous hands and a head which, by nature disproportionally large for his body, was magnified by dark medusa locks', it becomes natural to think of him not as a historical or literary figure, but as 'Vicky' or 'the Vickybird', as friends called him. Yet two shadows loom in which he has languished since his death. One is cast by Dylan Thomas, whom Neuburg discovered when editor of Poet's Corner in the *Sunday Referee*. The other by Aleister Crowley, the sorcerer who held sway over Vicky for seven years from 1906. Both felt 'love' for Vicky, while also holding him in the utmost contempt.

To Crowley, the 'sausage-lipped songster of Steyning' is a 'Caliban-like creature, a certain deformed and filthy abortion without moral character'. Thomas matches this vitriol, raging against a 'nineteenth-century crank' and 'the Creative Lifers', the put-down he applies to Vicky, his muse Runia Tharp and the poets of their circle.

What was it about Neuburg that inspired such scorn? His scruffy appearance? His penchant for Elizabethan-style clothing and speech? The extraordinary lengths he would go to when picking up litter or rescuing insects? Or was it, in the case of the Beast, high dudgeon because Neuburg threw off the shackles and turned off the money tap of family funds?

John Symonds, Crowley's first biographer, was the widowed Runia Tharp's lodger in London. Vicky's books on magic, still lining the living room shelves, played their part in sparking his fateful interest in Crowley. The result was *The Great Beast* (1951) in which Symonds did little to hide his distaste for his subject. In a similar vein, Jean Overton Fuller's *The Magical Dilemma of Victor Neuburg* (1965), though respectful of Crowley's erudition, portrays him as something unpleasant Neuburg got mixed up with – something for which she must apologise. Her antipathy was entirely typical of post-war Britain. Crowley was a monster, a charlatan, 'the King of Depravity', justifiably villainised.

Then in the 1960s, the first ripples of a sea change. With his use of drugs to expand consciousness and an esotericism that married East and West, the counterculture recognised in the Beast a fellow spirit. Symonds recorded his repugnance at this turnaround, a dismay that Overton Fuller must have shared.

How much more nonplussed would they be at the degree of rehabilitation Crowley has enjoyed in this millennium? Voted 73rd in BBC Two's 2002 poll of the *100 Greatest Britons*; well on his way, some consider, to becoming a national treasure. Today, scholars in the U.S. and Europe pore over his life and work – from his impact on astrology and Wicca to the eclectic range of 20th-century luminaries on whom he cast his spell.

Yet if anyone really knew Crowley and what he was up to it was Neuburg: no one travelled further or more perilously with the Beast. It was Neuburg who partnered Crowley in his most audacious Workings, imbued with more natural talent on the magical plane than anyone else he had ever known, according to the Beast.

The Neuburg of *Obsolete Spells* has settled down. He is in Steyning printing fine-looking books on the Vine Press. He is married and has a son. The turbulent years with Crowley are behind him; the period when he is once more 'in the swim' as editor of Poet's Corner is sometime ahead. But the past still casts a shadow. He comes across as feeling he has strayed from his true path and lives in fear that the Beast will prey on him.

Yet Neuburg does not recant or forswear the magic of his youth. He does not turn Catholic or take up golf. He publishes books that reflect his love of local lore and landscape. All the generosity of old is there. He is still progressive with a horror of the normal and is drawn to anarchy and to Vera Pragnell's Sanctuary, a community of sexually liberated free spirits. And there is still the magic: the esoteric musings of Ethel Archer's *Phantasy*, and that embodied in the collections of his own poetry:

> We who are burned by fire, buried in the earth,
> Drowned in the water, know the secret mirth,
> Sung to the stars by wandering elementals;
> The Soul of all things; the true transcendentals
> Deeper than death, above the need of birth.

His feelings for Crowley remain complicated. He is unsure if his former master is the foulest or greatest man who has ever lived. Despite all the damage their relationship did to his health, pocket, and sanity, he reviews the Beast's *Magick in Theory and Practice* (1929) and hails it as the greatest work on magic since the Renaissance.

Crowley displays no such generosity. The Beast, in fact, seems curiously unaffected by the visionary pyrotechnics of drugs and ritual magic; the lavatorial sexual practices; the followers who are drawn into his orbit and then burn up like meteors. He is multi-faceted it is true, an occult polymath, yet he remains resolutely one dimensional, ceaselessly on the make, prone to spite, conceit, and an adolescent urge to shock. Christopher Isherwood sampled the licentiousness of pre-Nazi Berlin in his company: "The truly awful thing about Crowley is that one suspects he didn't really believe in anything."

Neuburg, on the other hand, is a warm, flawed human being who works tirelessly to better the lot of others, especially fellow artists, and keeps faith with the magical, free-spirited royal road of his youth. Yet here we have a sneering Thomas, on Neuburg's *Sunday Referee*:

> A Sunday paper did its best
> To build a Sunday singing nest
> Where poets from their shelves could burst
> With trembling rhymes and do their worst
> To break the laws of man and metre
> By publishing their young excreta.

You pinch yourself and remember that Thomas was the loudest bird in the nest, regularly giving readings at Neuburg's home – the first steps on his path to greatness. Thomas, in fact, was playing to the gallery, unable to resist the temptation of sending up the foibles of his mentor. His true feelings for Vicky were more complex.

When Neuburg died in 1940, Dylan described him as 'a sweet wise man' and stated: 'he possessed many kinds of genius, and not least was his genius for drawing to himself, by his wisdom, graveness, great humour and innocence, a feeling of trust and love, that won't ever be forgotten'.

Obsolete Spells is proof of that.

VICTOR B.
NEUBURG AND
THE VINE PRESS

Nothing I can write or fashion
Will endure, but time must crumble
All my labour into dust.
Yet my work's not unavailing:
Now I write for others' seeing,
Others seeing, understanding
With a mightier sense than mine;
… Ever dying, recreating;
Changeless in reincarnating:
So the Spirit passes ever…

– Rold White, 'Poetic Reincarnation', Vine Press, 1929.

To be reborn and reborn again through poetry; that the ephemeral tokens one leaves on the earth might become the dawn of a dream-life after death through the works of others: this is the ecstasy of Victor Benjamin Neuburg. A poet and publisher, muse and mage, a man both out-of-time and of-the-moment, Neuburg played a central role in the artistic life of early-20th century England. And yet, within months of his early demise, he had all but vanished, his influence surviving only in the invisible bonds he helped to forge; the artistic lives he helped nurture.

He is known for his associations, as he should be. But it is neither his seven-year relationship with the Great Beast, the occultist Aleister Crowley, nor his discovery of the Great Poet, Dylan Thomas, that define the man, even if they may often describe him. In his work as a poet, and as an editor and publisher of poetry, Victor Neuburg struck coal as often as gold. Yet in his vision of the poetic life there was a beauty in the base and the dirty that shone just as brightly.

To see his life's work as a series of failures punctuated by moments of inspiration is to miss the point. To see what Neuburg accomplished requires looking not at individual strands, but at the spider's web. His genius was a modern one: as catalyst and curator, he took a world that gave him little solace and sculpted a new one for himself and his tribe.

Neuburg's adult life can be split into three parts, which (almost) neatly divide by decades into the '10s, '20s and '30s. From his start at Cambridge in 1906 until his recovery from the First World War in 1919, it was Aleister Crowley and his tantalising occult circle that dominated Neuburg's life. It was with Crowley and friends that he began his career as an editor and publisher, working to create *The Equinox*, modest house organ of Crowley's magical movement. In the 1930s, until his decline and eventual death in 1940, the London poetry world was Neuburg's domain, as he edited first Poet's Corner in the *Sunday Referee*, and, afterwards, his own arts, politics and poetry newsweekly, *Comment*. But in between the two, as London experienced the roaring twenties and the dawn of the modern world, Neuburg hunkered down in the sleepy Sussex town of Steyning with his own creation, The Vine Press.

There wasn't much to it. A hand-cranked printing press and a unique typeface, set in a room in a cottage, turned by Neuburg and his wife. But Vine Press became a tool its owner used to build the connections and networks upon which he thrived. From 1920 until 1930, Neuburg published an eclectic and eccentric collection of small-run books, none of which sold very many copies or are remembered today. What survives today – and, indeed, thrives – isn't the work of Vine Press, but its echo.

In Steyning, Neuburg was more than an anomaly, he was a sore thumb. He bounced through the streets of this prim-and-proper West Sussex town in his patchwork Norfolk jacket and knickerbockers, handsome despite his strange features – a head too big for his body, yet with lips too big for his head – carrying a stick and walking his roly-poly dog. He deftly defied the locals' desire to pigeonhole. His strange dress might have been acceptable, although more so in a wealthier man. But there was his manner – the flaneur's jaunt; the piercing laugh – and his language, filled with personal acronyms only he could understand (such as 'FrOG' – a Friend Of God, the agnostic Neuburg's joking term for a religious man), invented words ('ostrobogulous') and anachronistic references to Blake, Herodotus and Shelley. Still, this could've been overlooked if only the locals could make some sense of the comings-and-goings, the regular visitors of such odd extraction, and perhaps most of all, the question of *what he did all day*.

What he did was make books, broadsheets, cards and ephemera espousing a love of beauty – of beauty over anything else – that amounted to volleys in a cultural cold-war. And what he did, despite his removal from recognisable religion, was *believe*. Victor Neuburg believed wholeheartedly in his like-minded souls, the outsiders. His fellow travellers: the unacceptable. Victor Neuburg was modest and friendly to all, but deep down inside, he knew which side he was on.

'Vickybird', as he was called by his friends, never met a loser he didn't believe in; never found a cause without a glimmer of hope. He saw the good in criminals, the philosophy in lunatics, the strength in the broken and broken-hearted alike. And he built connections and catalysed change with an enthusiasm bordering on the manic. It was this belief in others despite all available evidence that proved his genius, built his world, and brought to him tragedy and destruction.

Early Life

Victor Benjamin Neuburg was born in London on Sunday 6 May 1883, to parents profoundly ill-prepared to welcome a child. Nine months and 11 days earlier, Jeannette Jacobs – one of several daughters of a successful businessman from a large and long-established London Jewish family – had married Carl (or Karl) Neuburg, an immigrant from Bohemia, in an arrangement made by their families. The pregnancy was a trying time: Carl threatened, cursed and beat Jeannette throughout, causing her to consider aborting the child more than once. It might not have come to that: at more than eight months' pregnant, Carl violently threw her against a mantelpiece, one of several acts abhorrent enough to warrant inclusion in Jeannette's extensive, disturbing divorce record. Within months of Victor's birth, Carl Neuburg had abandoned his wife and child for one of his multiple lovers, leaving them with little legacy but his surname and his cruelty.

With no father to speak of, Victor's childhood was spent surrounded by the tight-knit, traditional and religious Jacobs family: he, his mother, his grandmother and a flurry of aunts and uncles lived together in their home in Highbury, North London. The family business that his grandfather and uncles operated, Jacobs, Young and Westbury, dealt in everyday objects such as cane baskets and canvas sacks; among several sidelines was included, at one point, the sale of 'regulation'-sized canes for children's homes to use in corporal punishment. The business was successful enough not only to employ a significant portion of the family (a teenaged Victor would put in a few shifts himself, between school and university), but also to provide the household with two servants. When Rebecca Jacobs (Victor's grandmother) died in 1903, she left the modern equivalent of £1.5 million to her already comfortable children, and Jeannette and Victor departed London and moved south to Hove – the more 'respectable' west side of the coastal city of Brighton, Sussex.

Jeannette wasn't the only Jacobs to look southward: at around the same time, one of Victor's uncles purchased a cottage in Steyning, a few miles northwest of Hove, and handed it over as a Sussex bolthole for his sister, Theresa. Besides his mother, the young Victor's fondest relationship was with this doting 'Aunt Ti' whose attentions, and recently acquired second home in the South Downs, would become key to Victor's life. But in 1903, it was Hove that would be Victor's introduction to the county – and, in it, a literary theme that would prove potent for decades. Hove's twitching-curtains reputation and the shock of a smallish town after a lifetime in London, contrasted with the beauty of the nearby countryside and the glimmering sea, cemented in the young writer a love-hate relationship with Sussex. While he sometimes said Hove 'made him shudder', 20 years after his move there he would still write of it in the ecstatic manner of 21st-century psychogeographers, looking past the ignominy of its 'improved' state to something ancient and pagan that lingered and thrilled:

> Still the old airs! Vainly the fools 'improve'!
>> Thought lingers solidly; a lasting stain
>> Of thought, of dream, of love, of hate, of
>>> pain.
> After the centuries there is a grove
> Of oaks here still; white, furious figures move
>> Stormily to an old tempestuous strain;
>> Red drips remain where once were votives
>>> slain
> In the centuries before the birth of Hove.

> – Victor B. Neuburg, 'Hove Street', The Vine Press. 1921.

Neuburg's young adulthood was a period of wandering back and forth between various parts of London, Sussex and Cambridge, during which he stumbled into a literary life. Victor was very much a part of the stern, upright Jacobs family, but one might not have known it to see him. He was often ill, suffering spinal troubles from birth; he was scrawny of stature and lovably misshapen – the too-big head begins almost every contemporary's recollection of him; his arms were oddly bent, and his face practically outweighed his torso. He felt like an outsider, too. His family was *frum* – religiously observant and upstanding in the community. It was, to use Victor's own word, a 'fraub-y' way of being – stiflingly conservative and drab – and it wasn't how he wanted his life to be.

As he recalled to Jean Overton Fuller, a friend who would go on to write his biography (*The Magical Dilemma of Victor Neuburg*, Mandrake Press), one day while walking near his family's business on Borough High Street in South London he stumbled upon the offices of *The Freethinker* – an anti-religion publication founded, and at the time still edited, by the legendary secularist G.W. Foote. Thrilled at the idea that there was an alternative to the fraub-y life of *doing what's expected* that he saw in the demands of Jewish and Christian society, Neuburg took the new journal as manna from heaven. He had finally found those who kicked against the pricks.

And when Vickybird fell for something, he fell hard. Neuburg read and read and, soon, he wrote and wrote. From childhood he had lapped up Swinburne and Shakespeare, Austen and Keats. He began adding to the list: *The Freethinker* and *Agnostic Journal*, Walt Whitman and his English counterpart, Edward Carpenter; a particularly impactful read was the bombastically bleak 'City of Dreadful Night' by Bysshe Vanolis (aka James Thomson). The classics joined the fray and soon his attack on literature became twofold: successfully submitting pieces to *The Freethinker* and *Agnostic Journal*, and thereafter, at the age of 23, entering Cambridge University.

While his work at Cambridge was ostensibly towards a degree in modern languages at Trinity College, his passion for literature found its outlet less in his studies (he would graduate with a Third, the lowest degree he might've received) and more in his extracurricular activities. As a member of the Pan Society, he funnelled his freethinking into discussion of ideas both mystical and literary. (Pan, the wild, pastoral god of the

Greeks, was the go-to deity for Classicists of the decadent persuasion and would loom large in Neuburg's personal pantheon.) Besides participating in the Pan Society and Cambridge University Freethought Association, Neuburg continued submitting his poems and essays and, in the early spring of 1908, published his first book of poems – *A Green Garland*.

Comprised to no small extent of poems previously submitted to his two secularist outlets, *A Green Garland* is *almost* the kind of work one might expect a romantic in his twenties to write. And yet, there is – as one reviewer at the time put it – 'something in there; something which makes one feel certain there is more to come, whatever form it may take.' What shines through is Vickybird's belief in the power of poetry itself. Like in 'The First Poet', in which writers are all-but responsible for summoning the morning sun. The likes of Whitman and Shelley are praised as secular deities. Words echo like incantations – 'the dead, the dead…' 'asleep, asleep…' Already, here, is a sense of poetry as spellcasting.

That's not to say that *A Green Garland* made the literary world take notice. Almost no one did. But it was there: a book. The obsession had taken physical form.

Occult Circles

If literature was a distraction, then Crowley was a frenzy. When Neuburg met the infamous occult practitioner Edward Alexander 'Aleister' Crowley at Cambridge, the magician was already a household name – at least among any households Victor Neuburg would bother with. Crowley, a Trinity alum, found fertile recruiting grounds for his endeavours among the college's undergraduates and, in particular, the likes of the Pan Society. At the end of 1906, *Agnostic Journal* editor W.S. Ross (aka 'Saladin') died, and his funeral provided an opportunity for London's spiritual left-field to convene. Neuburg met Crowley aficionado, military strategist and fascist J.F.C. Fuller, who thought the young man ripe for magical undertakings and pointed his master in the right direction. Early in 1907, Crowley set off for one of his Cambridge visits and, in a moment that would change both men's lives forever, he walked into Neuburg's rooms and introduced himself.

At the time of their meeting, Aleister Crowley was an experienced 31 compared to Victor Neuburg's innocent 23. Crowley had been to India and Mexico, China and North Africa. He was a well-regarded Alpine mountaineer and one of Britain's early practitioners of yoga. He was immersed in all manner of arcane worship and decadent philosophy: he had studied alchemy and Islam; was actively publishing and actively bisexual; before meeting Neuburg, he had already joined, quit and effectively destroyed the famed Hermetic Order of the Golden Dawn.

Crowley, like Neuburg, had been raised in a conservative religious home – in his case a family of Plymouth Brethren – and he, too, was enthralled with the mad thrill and invulnerable confidence of his Blakean forebears. Crowley had used high-octane excess to get straight to the palace of wisdom, and once there, he kept on going. His appearance at Trinity was an explosion to Neuburg – as though this character had erupted from the pages of a book.

There is no doubt that Crowley wanted to find disciples for truly spiritual and magical purposes. But there were other reasons, too. Crowley's family had money – at least, in his youth. Having inherited a significant estate, Aleister burned through the cash in making his extensive early biography possible. By February, 1907, he was in a spectacularly failing marriage, broke and – for someone so deeply concerned and consumed with his self – rudderless.

Crowley, the master, offered keys to the doors of perception, sexuality, spirituality, and the decadent life. Neuburg, the disciple, quickly fell in love. But this disciple offered just as much to his teacher. His family's financial support, for example, was something of an aphrodisiac. And Crowley undoubtedly soon came to love Victor, too. His description of Neuburg on their first meeting is astute, and obviously caring. He describes Neuburg's fabulously unkempt appearance, his thick lips ('three times too large for him … put on hastily as an afterthought'), his jittery behaviour and unsettling laugh. But to Crowley, Victor was also 'extraordinarily well read, overflowing with exquisitely subtle humour, and … one of the best natured people that ever trod this planet.'

Crowley also noted the younger man's desire for the outré:

> He was a mass of nervous excitement, having reached the age of twenty-five [sic] without learning how to manage his affairs. He had been prevented from doing so, in fact, by all sorts of superstitions about the terrible danger of leading a normal wholesome life.

As Neuburg fell under the spell, Crowley's reading list joined (and perhaps supplanted) that of his Cambridge studies. Some of this list wouldn't surprise any university student (Plato, Shakespeare, Rabelais) while other entries must have been rather eccentric for Cambridge in 1907 – texts by theosophists and Rosicrucians; the *Bhagavad Gita* and *The Book of the Dead*. With Crowley coming to address the Pan Society in a series of scandal-laced lectures, there was a growing confusion over who was directing Neuburg's studies. It didn't take long for that fog to clear: he was Crowley's student, and Cambridge was an afterthought.

Neuburg must have been aware of his own bisexuality before 1907, but was also utterly without experience, and possibly a virgin however one looked at it – a situation Crowley relieved twice over. Within a month of meeting, the men were sexual partners, and not long after, the older man would cajole Neuburg into liaison with a Parisian lady of the night. There was unquestionably a tenderness to Crowley's feelings about Neuburg, but that tenderness was overcome by something else. He grew to despise the young man's innocence and bewilderment combined with what he saw as a natural brilliance – what Crowley called, 'an altogether extraordinary capacity for Magic'; in particular, spiritualism and clairvoyance. So much so, in fact, that the mage believed Neuburg was unable to control his capacity for communion with spirits and demons, and would later write that this openness to the spirit world may have proved 'finally fatal to him'.

Over the course of Neuburg's Cambridge career, their relationship grew more intense. There were positive aspects to this – they travelled, from decadence in Paris to a walking holiday in Spain and adventures in North Africa. And then there was the beginning of the guru's manipulation – from simple things like the reading list and Crowley's demands of discipline, to the breaking down of Neuburg's sense of self, as when his 'Sweet Wizard' tricked Victor into believing a Parisian model was in love with him, only to reveal her as one of Crowley's own lovers.

The summer after finishing at Cambridge, Neuburg went for his 'magical retirement' at Crowley's estate on Loch Ness, Boleskine House. By this time, the Wizard had formed his own new magical order – known as the A∴A∴ and dedicated to a kind of spiritual individualism, albeit by gaining knowledge through a rigorous series of guru-opened doors. Neuburg was one of the first members of the group and, through his dedication to the master, may have been part of its inspiration. Now, with his magical name *Frater Omnia Vincam*, Neuburg would take the next step in his training: ten days isolated at Boleskine House performing rituals, reading, learning discipline both spiritual and physical.

Along with the training came abuse. Crowley whipped Neuburg with stinging nettles and made him sleep naked on gorse in the Highland air. He grew increasingly rough in both actions and words, his professed interest in Jewish mysticism giving way to a basic and vociferous anti-semitism. (Jean Overton Fuller would later pin some of Neuburg's lifelong health struggles, including the tuberculosis from which he died, to the abuses of this period.)

·/.

After this retirement, Neuburg, now Crowley's official magical squire, was to join his master on a journey to Algiers and into the desert. There they would follow the magical recipes of the sixteenth-century English court astrologer John Dee. Crowley shaved Neuburg's head but for two dyed-red horns of hair. Crowley, at least once, attacked Neuburg with a knife during their rituals in what was likely a drug-fuelled assault. Neuburg's job was to record all the magical proceedings. This included taking his master's dictated notes and letters in which he not only derided Neuburg, but described the secretary's homosexual acts, generating what could've been, at the time, a criminal confession in Neuburg's own hand. Meanwhile, Victor's family was paying for it all, with Crowley either sweet-talking or bullying them in a cycle of borrow-and-spend, at one point sending word from Algeria to North London to send '£500 or you will never see your son again'.

Most importantly, it was in the desert that Crowley first joined sex with magick, opening his eyes to the possibilities of ritualistic sex. In a spur-of-the-moment addition to one of their rituals, Crowley and Neuburg built an altar on a desert hill, on top of which Crowley 'sacrificed himself' in an act of submission to his disciple. This sex magick would become part of Crowley's magical signature, the physical acts intended to consecrate the actors through sexual intensity, destroying shame and unleashing raw, pure magic.

The trip to the desert would become infamous for the rumour that Crowley successfully transformed Neuburg into an animal: a camel, a goat, even a zebra. Some of Neuburg's friends were convinced that, at the very least, he *believed* this had happened – although when his young friend, the writer Arthur Calder-Marshall, asked him about the rumours a decade later, he laughed them off. The Vine Press author Vera Pragnell, however, described hearing his memories of being cursed as a goat as 'chilling'.

The most infamous, and in their minds most magically successful, of the couple's rituals was what came to be known as The Paris Working. For six weeks at the beginning of 1914 they sequestered themselves in a Paris apartment, took drugs and had ritualistic sex. It was, certainly for Neuburg, the apotheosis of his magical career; it's possible Crowley thought it was his own, too, although he of course would continue on related paths for three more decades.

The workings involved a lot of sex and opium. There was sadism and masochism on behalf of each of the partners: Victor was whipped and cut for ritualistic purposes, but he was also usually the 'active' partner (as Jean Overton Fuller puts it) in their sexual acts. In one instance, Crowley made Neuburg sit in the audience with a few others while a mutual friend sodomised the 'Sweet Wizard'. For sure, Crowley's account of the experiment also contains more otherworldly moments: possession by ancient gods, past-life regressions, conversations with astral forces. And yet it doesn't seem particularly obvious, to those of us reading a century later, what magick was accomplished. Perhaps such drug-fuelled experiences always read as rather lacklustre after the fact – regardless of how profound they seemed to the active parties.

Like many of Crowley's magical enterprises in these years, there was an element to Paris of overcoming shame through sex – perhaps the great success of the workings was a fulfilling, profound rejection (destruction, in fact) of each man's orthodox religious upbringing. No matter what shame and bourgeois mediocrity came before or comes after, they seemed to be saying, *we'll always have Paris.*

The most important development to come of the Paris Working was the disillusion of Neuburg's love for Crowley. In a moment of clarity, the older man told his partner, 'I am always unlucky for you … you always have to sacrifice everything for my love.' Neuburg must have finally recognised this as truth. There's little doubt that he had already soured on the relationship. Perhaps he had outgrown the infatuation; perhaps he had recognised that after everything he had given – the time, the attention, the money, the blood – he was still the butt of the joke, never an equal.

In February of 1914, the two returned to England. In May, they spoke for the final time, and upon their parting, Crowley cursed his former lover – a curse in which Neuburg believed completely, regardless of its true potential. Theirs had certainly been the key relationship in Neuburg's life – it opened doors and opened eyes, and led him on a path that might've been unimaginable without Crowley. But it was a turning point in other ways, too. Always imbalanced, at times abusive both physically and emotionally, it was the relationship of cult-leader and devoted victim as much as two lovers or friends.

One insight into their life together can be found in the 1911 UK census. The census form, completed by each head-of-household and noting any present in their house on the chosen date (in this case, Sunday 2 April, 1911) is meant to capture a snapshot of the country. Crowley's home, 124 Victoria St., London, SW, includes Neuburg on that date. Crowley lists his own occupation as 'Poet', and Victor as his employee – 'Private Chaplain'. Finally, Victor Benjamin Neuburg is noted by the head-of-household as suffering from infirmity number four on the form's list: 'Imbecile or Feeble-minded. Congenital [idiot].'

It's difficult to attribute, as some have done, Neuburg's terminal lung disease in 1940 to sleeping on gorse or Algerian sex antics 30 years previous, but the direct line between Crowley's mental cruelty and manipulation and Neuburg's decline is more certain. One of Crowley's many biographers, Martin Booth, posits that, 'In Neuburg Crowley was not only sinning but manufacturing his own custom-made sinner' – destroying his own, and his subject's, religious upbringing through the magical transformation of an innocent into something else.

In this he was only partially successful. He unleashed Neuburg's libertine self, a sexually permissive and artistically lavish soul – a creative rebel, rather than a destructive one. But Neuburg, by almost every account of him, retained his belief in the beauty of others and of the world around him. And even those few who came to despise him (and there were at least some) did so because his inability to cope with the real world caused them heartbreak and trouble, not because he willingly caused them harm.

The years he spent with Crowley were filled with enormous joy as well, and alongside the abuse, Neuburg gained invaluable knowledge and relationships that he would draw on for the rest of his life. There was *The Equinox*, the occult periodical that Crowley began publishing for his A∴ A∴ in 1909. Neuburg was a contributor to most issues of the first volume, and the part-subject of Crowley's own infamous contribution, 'The Vision and the Voice', regarding their time in Algeria. In late 1910, the *Equinox* published Neuburg's second book of poetry, *The Triumph of Pan*. But perhaps the more telling moment for the poet would be his role as an editor on the journal: he was working, not as a poet, but as the channel for the work of others. He was editing, and indeed publishing, for the first time.

Neuburg was deeply affected by the large artistic, literary and spiritual circle that he entered during his Crowley years. Imagine Victor Neuburg's concept of 'family': he was raised in a household of many, and yet was also the only child of a single mother. He saw his childhood home as both stifling and a safety net. Its relationships were close and vital, yet also chilly and insufficient. Through his freethought and his poetry, and then through Crowley, he had come into a world that seemed right – relationships built on invigorating ideas, and actions that paid little heed to convention. He had found a family that made more sense.

Friends of Eleusis

If there was a point around which this sense of family coalesced, it might've been the Rites of Eleusis. This 1910 series of rituals-slash-performances (and the at-home precursors, which sometimes included viewers) in which, among other things, Neuburg excelled at dance, included among its performers and audience many of the characters who would influence Neuburg's sphere for years to come. Likewise there were his own poems in *The Triumph of Pan*. Each of these is dedicated to an individual, including most of the early members of the A∴ A∴ as well as the artists, writers and cheerleaders Neuburg had encountered between his arrival at Cambridge and the book's 1910 publication. It amounts to a roster of those appearing in Neuburg's life at the time.

One *Freethinker* friendship that would prove both unshakeable and, possibly, life-saving was William Edward Hayter Preston (occasionally, 'Teddie'; more often simply Hayter Preston). The two men shared an excitable love of philosophy, poetry, art and rebellious thought, but on first glance they must have been a strange pair: while

Neuburg was fey and dainty, bumbling and odd, Preston was a tall, physically confident ex-rugby player, as at home in the boxing ring as an art gallery. Neuburg introduced his friend to Crowley, beginning Preston's long and tumultuous interest in the occult. Other questionable figures loomed larger in Preston's world, notably Ezra Pound, for whom he had a fascination and high regard until the two wound up on opposite sides of the fascist question.

Neuburg would cross paths with Preston again quite fortuitously in 1917, when the poet landed in France for his stint in the army. Upon arrival at Abbeville, Neuburg – whose incompetence at all matters of soldiering brought laughter and some sympathy from fellow soldiers – was surprised to be placed under arrest, only to discover it was by order of the Sergeant, Hayter Preston. Thanks to his old friend, Neuburg spent the rest of the war lighting fires for the commanding officers and translating poetry from the French while Preston typed it up.

After the war, Preston and Neuburg would live together in Steyning and launch The Vine Press. Soon, Preston would drift back to London and become a well-established journalist, writing about everything from art and literature to sport, and a poet. His editorship at *The Referee* (later, *Sunday Referee*) and his columns as 'Vanoc II' became important parts of London's literary swim and anti-fascist political agenda. In the 1930s it's arguable he saved Neuburg's life again by giving him control of Poet's Corner in that publication, the venue through which Vickybird celebrated his muses by discovering and publishing poets both legendarily great and abominably bad.

Two others are named as having been present in Crowley's rooms at 124 Victoria Street when the 1911 national census-taker called. Neuburg was listed as a 'visitor', as were Eugene J. Wieland (known as 'Bunko' and listed as Crowley's 'Private Secretary'), and his wife, Ethel Wieland. Twenty years later, Eugene Wieland would be long dead and Crowley an unhappy memory. But Neuburg would still be close with Ethel, and published a book under her maiden name, Ethel Archer, as the final Vine Press production.

The Wielands had become tantalised by Crowley's world, if perhaps initially with some trepidation, at an early, drug-laced performance of the Rites at Victoria Street. By the time of the census, the two were entwined with the Crowley circle. She was a regular contributor to *The Equinox*, and her book of poems, *The Whirlpool*, would be published by the imprint soon after Neuburg's *The Triumph of Pan*. She would fall out with Crowley but remain close to Neuburg, and after 1915, when her husband was killed in the First World War, she concentrated her efforts on poetry and prose spawned by those formative few years. She proved an ally to Neuburg and Vine Press at *The Occult Review*, for which she wrote, and he, in turn, published a wide-ranging collection of her poems under the title *Phantasy* in 1930.

In something of a backwards manner, the prolific novelist and essayist Arthur Calder-Marshall met Neuburg through Crowley. A teenager living in Steyning when he met 'the Poet', Calder-Marshall came to him because of the tantalising tales of the infamous mage. The young writer became fascinated with all things magical, and used his connection with Neuburg to wend his way deeper into London's underworld, finally befriending the Beast, as documented in his excellent memoir, *The Magic of My Youth*. He helped rejuvenate Neuburg's poetry thrill, too, inviting his mentor to speak at Oxford when Vickybird's passion was dulling. Long after Neuburg's death, Calder-Marshall would keep his name alive through a series of articles and essays related to literature and the esoteric in which he mentioned Vickybird as often as he could.

Philip Heseltine, professionally known as Peter Warlock, was a composer whose work is still performed and studied today. He was fascinated by magic and by Crowley and Neuburg in particular, and joined the Order, befriending the poet. He became an ally of Neuburg's throughout the Vine Press years, collaborating with him to set several of his publications to music, until Warlock's death (likely by suicide) in 1930 at the age of 36.

Other veterans of the Crowley-related circle would appear throughout Neuburg's life, primarily fellow outcasts and self-exiles like Preston and Archer. The mononymic enigma Cremers, who claimed to have known Jack the Ripper; the 'Queen of Bohemia', Nina Hamnett, who wrote of Neuburg in her book *Laughing Torso*; the artist Austin Osman Spare, who was still in close communication with Neuburg up to the poet's death; musician Leila Waddell, a key performer in Crowley's rituals, who stayed in contact with not just Victor but the extended Neuburg family for some time.

And then there was Jeanne, the ghost that was always there, following Victor, 'like a person just gone': Ione, as Ezra Pound wrote of her, 'Dead the long year'.

Born Jeanne Heyse in London, 1890, to a Dutch-French father and Irish mother, Jeanne transformed first into Joan Hayes and then, ditching any nominal proximity in favour of artistic flair, Ione de Forest. A RADA-trained dancer and artist, in 1910 she departed the successful West End debut production of Maeterlinck's *The Blue Bird* and joined the troupe for the Rites of Eleusis. By that time she and Victor were lovers, and passionately so – or, certainly, he was. Nina Hamnett would later write of the couple in *Laughing Torso*, calling them, 'The poet and the beautiful girl': 'She had golden eyes and the most perfect eyebrows; she had long black hair down to her waist. He wrote hundreds and hundreds of poems to her.'

Crowley's spell over Victor was beginning to break, and – seeing the cracks – he was enraged. This rage created a rift between Victor and Jeanne, and in 1911 she married Wilfred Merton, the stepson of the fabulously wealthy Anglo-German industrialist Zachary Merton. (It's possible, even likely, that they met through Victor, who knew Merton in his Cambridge years and had dedicated poems to each of them in *The*

Triumph of Pan.) The marriage failed at the first hurdle, and six months later she had moved into her Rossetti Studios space in Chelsea and was seeing Victor again.

On the 2 August, 1912, Jeanne Heyse dressed herself elegantly, sat down on the sofa in her studio and shot herself through the heart with a mother-of-pearl pistol. It was meticulously planned: she had purchased the gun two weeks earlier and posted a one-line letter to her husband that morning, 'You have killed me. Jeanne.' She told Nina Hamnett she'd be leaving on a journey and had some things for her, and to stop by that day. Hamnett arrived to a note on the door instructing her to let herself in, whereupon she discovered the body. Jeanne had threatened to kill herself many times. This time, she kept her word.

In the ensuing hearings and their drooling news coverage the name Victor B. Neuburg was never mentioned, but there is no doubt the triangle between him, Heyse and Merton – plus Crowley's ever-present menace – was close to the suicide's shattered heart. Arthur Calder-Marshall certainly claims it was. According to his telling, Heyse was pregnant with Victor's child, and she and her lover argued viciously the night before the suicide. She threatened to kill herself, once again, and this time Victor told her to go ahead. In *The Magic of My Youth*, Calder-Marshall theorises that Neuburg was under the spell of Mars, put there by Crowley – or, just as potently, *believed* himself to be. Regardless, if the fight happened it was a rare moment of rage for the poet, and with a very unfortunate target. And even if it didn't, there is little doubt that the tragedy stayed with Neuburg forever.

Despite their Paris Working, the break between Neuburg and Crowley couldn't be reversed after Heyse. Later in life, on the rare occasions he would speak of her, Neuburg would sometimes directly blame Heyse's death on the magician. As Crowley scholar Gary Lachman points out, the Beast not only did nothing to dispel this but actively engaged it as a possibility, writing in *Magick in Theory and Practice* that, 'The Master Therion once found it necessary to slay a Circe who was bewitching brethren. He merely walked to the door of her room, and drew an Astral T … with an astral dagger. Within 48 hours she shot herself.' Crowley created the circumstances, the actors believed him responsible, and he claimed responsibility. Is that not, in fact, a spell well cast?

It was Hayter Preston who helped Neuburg finalise his split from Crowley. Neuburg had seen the circle he adored – that of which he sang praises in *The Triumph of Pan* – fall into darkness, anger, depression and death. His community, his family, had failed him utterly. By the end of 1914 Victor Neuburg had quit Crowley, his order, and his grasp. He fled the 'scene', to friends in the West Country and, not long after – and against his interests – he joined the army and headed for his fateful reunion with Hayter Preston.

Victor B. Neuburg, only son of an abused and abandoned mother, found himself in tatters. For seven years he had lived in and out of a mentally and physically abusive relationship. He had seen his lover, possibly pregnant with their child, take her own life. By the Autumn of 1915, Eugene Wieland was dead too. Neuburg's own war experience, while not battle-hardened, would've seen him surrounded by death at Abbeville, through which the front line's dead and wounded were siphoned.

Inevitably, Neuburg broke down.

Steyning and The Vine Press

St Cuthman was an Anglo-Saxon shepherd who famously converted to Christianity along with some of his Sussex brethren in the 7th or 8th century and who, much more famously, carried his mother around in a wheelbarrow. Destitute, fatherless, his mother paralysed, he set out, relying on the generosity of others. His wheelbarrow broke at a spot where the River Adur cut through the foot of the chalk hills of the South Downs, the rolling hills that stretch along England's southern coast. There, Cuthman stayed; he built a church, and spawned the town of Steyning.

Steyning sits in an enviable location. For centuries it was a port, and a prosperous one at that, and it maintained its market, important for the rich agricultural work going on for miles around its hub. And it has long attracted visitors due to its gorgeous stretch of the South Downs. Above the town is Chanctonbury Ring, a high point on the Downs and site of an Iron Age hill fort, renowned for its views over sea and downs as well as for its crowning glory: a splendid ring of beech trees, planted in the 18th century. Romano-British pagans built temples there and rumours abound of Druidic sacrifice before them. In fact, the whole area around Chanctonbury and nearby Cissbury Ring is something of a 'legend landscape': even in the 21st century it has given rise to mystery tales ranging from covens of witches to ghosts to levitation by UFO.

A stone's throw from the church Cuthman founded, Victor B. Neuburg put down his struggles and, like the Saint, sought roots and solace in Steyning. Vine Cottage is a longish frontage halfway between the High Street and the church, sandwiched between an ancient timber-framed cottage and the Norfolk Arms pub. There's something about it that compels attention, despite its low setting and eponymous beard of vines. When Neuburg's uncle purchased it, and gave it to Aunt Ti, it must have seemed the quietest place in the world to the Jacobs family, to which London bustle was a generations-long norm. Steyning wasn't isolated by any stretch: the train service from the local station, a short walk from Vine Cottage, was good enough for some to commute to London for work even then. In the course of his years there, Steyning changed. Author Rupert Croft-Cooke compares visiting in the later '20s to his initial stays a half-decade earlier, pointing out that 'by now the traffic through Steyning made it impossible to open a window on the street'. But to Neuburg, after Cambridge and London; after Crowley and Abbeville and stints in two post-war convalescent hospitals; after all the drama and trauma, it must have been heavenly.

Aunt Ti gave him possession of Vine Cottage sometime around 1919, and Neuburg and his stalwart companion, Hayter Preston, moved in soon after. Perhaps it was meant to be temporary, a halfway house between the army hospital and the 'real world'. Or perhaps it was all part of a plan hatched during long nights of poetry in Abbeville: they should start a press. Not one to take over the world, but to be smuggled into it; something that could be coarse and beautiful at the same time. A press making books and poems that might be handed around under dim lights, and whispered of by the likes of the Pan Society.

Victor lived off a small allowance from his family – what was left, that is, after Crowley's seven-year squeeze. Aunt Ti provided the home at Vine Cottage. And now she sank some more into the Victor biz: with her backing, he and Preston bought a printing press and an anachronistic, unique typeface. The Vine Press was born.

Before there were even words to set with it, that typeface must have thrilled Neuburg. The initial Vine Press books, printed on this machine and with this type, were loaded with serifs; they had looping double-o's (like in 'book' or 'look') and a connected 'st' that sings of pastoral times. Occasionally this causes issues: the tiny, invisible 'o' and normal-sized 'u' in the word CoUNTRY, for example, renders an altogether different word. But it is undoubtedly a magnificent font in which to print.

Immediately, for the Vickybird, it was back: that indescribable, indeed magical, joy at poetry. Since *The Triumph of Pan*, he had published little. His most ambitious work from the period, a book-length poem entitled 'The New Diana', was written in 1912 but remained unpublished in his lifetime. With the means of production in hand, in 1920 he set to printing, but even then, not his own work. In fact, thanks to a series of pseudonyms and anonymous publications, The Vine Press never published any books directly attributed in print to the name Victor B. Neuburg.

Arthur Calder-Marshall conjectured that this anonymity was down to Jeanne Heyse, her tragedy bringing the poet such shame that he wanted to keep his name quiet and avoid painful queries. There is also evidence that his relationship with Crowley had earned him a blacklisting in some publishing quarters, which may have contributed to the desire for a private press. More plausible is the mention by Rupert Croft-Cooke of an agreement with Aunt Ti. That Neuburg might have been given the money for the press on condition of capitalism – that it be used to print books to sell, rather than to become a mere vehicle for his own endless (and, in the family's experience, costly) literary ambitions – seems plausible. (This anonymity survived the Vine Press lifetime in name only, and by 1925 his anonymous work was being attributed, at least in advertisements, to Victor B. Neuburg.)

So, among the first few books The Vine Press published, from 1920–1922, were collections including anonymous verse – Scots ballads, English broadsides, folk tales – and known works from the periods and poets Neuburg admired: John Keats, Aphra Behn, Nicholas Udall. There were translations of classical lyrics and, in at least one case, a contemporary poet, and there were lots and lots of bawdy pieces geared towards reddening faces. Besides books, there were commercial endeavours – printing cards and leaflets; within a few years, Vine Press was selling pens and whatever else.

The Vine Press was far from alone in such work in the 1920s – a kind of golden age for small presses in England – and inspiration was close at hand. Just up the road was Ditchling, Sussex, and Eric Gill's infamous artist's colony, which had recently established its St Dominic's Press. The founding of The Society of Wood Engravers in 1920 influenced the artistic direction of the private presses: Robert Gibbings, one of the organisation's founders, would start Golden Cockerel Press in the mid-'20s, making books in a style similar to The Vine Press with writers and artists including Gill, Enid Clay, John Nash and David Jones. Hayter Preston's books for The Bodley Head (*The House of Vanities* with Claud Lovat Fraser; *Windmills* with Frank Brangwyn) are further examples of the moment's style.

Besides printing beloved old verse, there were also plenty of poems by Victor B. Neuburg in the early Vine Press; they just didn't bear his name. The second book printed, *Swift Wings*, was comprised entirely of Neuburg's own work – poems about the Sussex landscape – but is simply left unattributed, its 'author' mentioned in the Publisher's Note as though someone else. But while the author isn't mentioned, its dedicatee is at least open to an educated guess: 'TO KAROG.'

Vickybird had known Kathleen Rose Goddard for some time, but when their relationship began is less clear. Born in 1892, she was nearly a decade his junior. By 1911 she was working in the post office in Hove, and during Victor's visits there after Jeanne's death in 1912, she would have been the young woman behind the counter. By 1920 she had left for a job he helped her acquire as secretary to the dancer and choreographer Margaret Morris, at the latter's school in London. By most accounts she had less artistic inclination than many in Vickybird's world, but she was important enough to Morris for her to join the dancer's summer school in Pourville, France, in August of 1921. In November of that year, Kathleen and Victor were married in London; in April, 1922, she left the Margaret Morris School for good and became a permanent fixture at Vine Cottage.

By then Hayter Preston had removed himself from the Cottage. In 1922 The Bodley Head published his book of prose poems, *The House of Vanities*, with posthumous illustrations by the artist Claud Lovat Fraser, who had died aged 31 the previous summer. It would've made a brilliant

Vine Press book, and seems to come from the same mindset: even the illustrations are strikingly similar in style to the debut from Vine Press, *Lillygay*. But by then, and likely with Preston's initial charismatic help, Neuburg had a few books under his belt, and had begun to assemble a circle of mostly young and eager fellow travellers.

Despite Steyning's decorous reputation, Neuburg found many of his co-conspirators among the locals. Foremost to the enduring legacy of The Vine Press were the West brothers, Dennis (b. 1883), Eric (b. 1897) and Percy (b. 1898). They came from a large and well-established Steyning family: between their siblings (besides the three brothers there were seven more) and their forebears, the family's tendrils extended into most segments of Steyning life, from cow-men to innkeepers and, soon, the printer's shop that would remain central to the town's High Street all the way through to the 1990s. All three boys were back from active duty in the First World War, alive if not entirely intact (Eric lost part of a leg) and looking for a safer kind of adventure.

Beginning with the first Vine Press book in 1920, the brothers made woodcut illustrations for Neuburg. Eric and Percy worked on *Lillygay* while Dennis made work for 1921's *Songs of the Groves* and 1922's *Larkspur*, but the work is similar enough to be seen as a whole body, and it is a fascinating one. Just as so many of the poems in these books originated in broadsides, penny ballads and collections like *The Dancing Master*, the Wests' woodcuts emulate the illustrations that accompanied those: rough block cuts of maidens, landscapes and portraits; unmannered, outsider black-and-white prints. And in their simplicity they gain an eeriness that's difficult to either pinpoint or dispel. The distance of a century helps: today, early books from The Vine Press give off a sensual leer and a slight air of threat that belies their jolly, bawdy origins, yet – I think – brings the reader to exactly the spot that Neuburg intended.

There were others, as well. Beatrice Linda Stanbrough, from Hove, was 27 when she contributed the cover art of a windmill to Neuburg's *Swift Wings*. Eve Rice was a local Steyning woman who, at barely 24, made the wood-cut illustrations for Princess Ouroussoff's book *Before the Storm*. Merton Davis was an inventor whose 'Merton Davis pen' was available for purchase through The Vine Press: in 1932 he and Eve Rice married, one of the happier meetings the Press conferred.

Two unsung heroes of the early Vine Press are Kathleen Neuburg and Kensett bookbinders of Brighton. Kathleen was never directly credited in a Vine Press book, and Jean Overton Fuller and Arthur Calder-Marshall go out of their way to point out her non-artistic – and financially oriented – way of life. But Mrs Neuburg was a key part of the production process for Vine Press: contemporaries commented that the couple seemed at their happiest while printing and cutting pages, often late into the night. And while the two Neuburgs printed the books, it was the bindery of Kensett in Brighton (still operating today) that put those pages between the boards, producing the gold-embossed spines for which the first Vine Press editions are known among collectors.

Beginning in 1922 with Rupert Croft-Cooke's *Songs of a Sussex Tramp*, The Vine Press began publishing other living writers, drawing largely from the Sussex area. It had the joint prospect of being a business move and, potentially, satisfying the 'deal' with his family, while also allowing Neuburg to continue producing books of poetry – at least at the speed a hand-operated press allowed. But as he had shown in his family's business, Neuburg didn't have a capitalist bone in his body – in fact, in his autobiography, Croft-Cooke aptly describes Neuburg's business acumen as non-existent. Rupert Croft-Cooke was only 17 when he sent his poems to Neuburg, blind. (He would go on to have a prolific career as a writer and a fascinating, if often difficult, life: he spent six months in prison for homosexuality in the 1950s, and subsequently left Britain, disgusted with the bigotry and fearing for his freedom.)

More books followed: Worthing businessman Ernest Osgood Hanbury's nature poems may have been a strictly commercial endeavour, while young army veteran G.D. Martineau, another Sussex man, became the first writer to have two Vine Press books published in his name. An exiled Russian 'princess' and two historian sisters with local connections were also part of the mix. The Vine Press had begun with a clear intention – to print books with poetic integrity which might, also, sell – but by the mid-'20s it had begun to swerve into somewhat anarchic territory.[1]

Besides his authors, artists and other book-related fellows, Victor Neuburg began to build into a circle the few, but influential, left-wing political minds that the Steyning area had to offer. In 1926 he befriended the legendary septuagenarian anarchist W.C. Owen, back from his time in California and Mexico, who would come to live his final days at Vine Cottage a few years later. Soon after the general strike in May of that year, Owen wrote that he had 'stirred' both Victor and Kathleen to the anarchist cause. Another strike ally was the future Marxist historian A.L. Morton, who worked at Steyning Grammar School and gravitated to Vine Cottage. Morton would remain a staunch Neuburg ally through the rest of his life. And it was from Vine Cottage, too, that Labour's prospective candidate Walter Raeburn based his work in the Worthing region while

---

1   One intriguing off-catalogue piece of the Vine Press legacy is *The Way of a Virgin*, a collection of folk tales, all sexual in nature, excerpted and translated from a variety of sources by a pair of author/editors named as L. and C. Brovan. It was almost certainly made at least in part by Neuburg, possibly with The Vine Press, though it is attributed to 'The Brovan Society', and no mention of Neuburg, his collaborator(s) or the Press are included.

down from his home in London, along with Neuburg's friend, the future radio producer Eric J. King Bull. (Throughout the decade's second half, Vickybird was an active party member, with Vine Cottage the hub for Steyning's few Labour activists. In 1928 he was elected to the Horsham and Worthing Labour Party Committee.)

The Sanctuary

Without question the most important element in Neuburg's social, artistic and political circle in Steyning was the Sanctuary. It was at this utopian community near Storrington, West Sussex, that Neuburg's *Freethinker* mindset enjoyed a happy collision with anarchist, humanist and sexually-liberated philosophies and actions. It is there that he met Owen, as well as a slew of figures that would loom large over Victor Neuburg's life in Steyning and beyond.

Hidden away in the woods off the main Storrington-Washington road beneath Chanctonbury Ring's northern escarpment, around three-dozen adults and half as many children lived permanently with a rotating cast of guests. Their philosophy of life was significantly different to that of the surrounding area: as one tabloid disparagingly put it, there were 'no moral restrictions … all may enter freely, be they black or white, atheist or Christian.' Communists and anarchists; foreigners and freethinkers; poets, pagans and nudists – all the best tabloid paydirt found a home at the Sanctuary. As one might imagine, it was incredibly popular. In 1929 the community claimed a waiting list of 300 names looking to move in.

The Sanctuary proved worthy of its name to Vickybird in the 1920s. Arthur Calder-Marshall describes the poet's transformation traveling the short journey there from Steyning:

> His whole manner changed as we boarded the bus and drew out of Steyning ... In Steyning, when he was indoors he was the drone-like father; and when he went down the street he was the mad Poet. But in the Sanctuary he and the Queen held court like Oberon and Titania. He was a visiting potentate, a poet whose poems had actually been published, a publisher who actually published poems.

'The Queen', as Vickybird would certainly have considered her, was the Sanctuary's founder, Vera Pragnell. The daughter of a very successful businessman and patriot, she had turned her notable energies to helping the downtrodden and founding a community that saw everyone as worthwhile. 'Goodness yes,' she would help anyone, she wrote, 'it may be Christ! Sometimes the disguise seems inches thick.' Her significant inheritance went to purchase the land on which the community was built.

The Queen's likeminded subjects became integral to Neuburg's Steyning life, and many of them remained in his orbit afterwards. Dennis Earle, her soon-to-be husband, was another early settler, and had previously had a professional and personal relationship with one of Neuburg's idols, the sexual-liberation advocate Edward Carpenter. Regular visitor Dion Byngham, of the Order of Woodcraft Chivalry – a group akin to a semi-pagan, pacifist Boy Scouts – published Victor's poetry in that organisation's newsletters. Byngham and his girlfriend were avowed naturists, and brought the Sanctuary its first press attention when they enjoyed a nude ramble along the nearby Downs.

It was at the Sanctuary that Victor got to know the psychologist Dr Harold Dinely Jennings 'Rold' White, who would go on to publish two volumes with The Vine Press. Dr H.D. Jennings White, as he was professionally known, was a fascinating polymath: a psychologist, philosopher and writer whose interests aligned with Neuburg's on numerous subjects, all filed loosely under counter-cultural thinking. White seems to have been born with a fully formed philosophy: as a young man, his religious and political convictions had him spend the war years in Wormwood Scrubs prison and a series of labour camps, arrested as a conscientious objector. It had a transformative impact, dedicating him to a life in pursuit of freedom and mental, physical and spiritual health, although he rarely spoke of it: his poems for Vine Press, many written while imprisoned, bear no mention of their origin; he only told his daughter of his C.O. ordeal on his deathbed.

In the 1920s, it was White's then-radical views on sex that brought him some small national attention. He thought neither masturbation nor homosexuality were evil or, in fact, bad at all; he even had the gall to believe that women should *enjoy sex*. And he believed in rehabilitation, rather than mere punishment, as the right course to take with criminals.

Neuburg obviously appreciated Jennings White greatly, publishing two books of his poetry and then continuing to lure him into Vickybird projects throughout the 1930s. But the trail isn't a simple one. Like so many of the people associated with The Vine Press, Jennings White didn't stick to a single name. Dr H.D. Jennings White was the psychologist and philosopher; Arthur Beldare was his pseudonym for painting and music; and for poetry, an old family nickname: Rold White.

Perhaps most important of all, it was likely through the Sanctuary that Vickybird met Runia MacLeod. No one played the name game like Runia. Through her marriages to two artists (Leslie Augustus Bellin-Carter and Charles Julian Tharp) and her disdain for all-things patriarchy, she wound up with at least a half-dozen names both legal and *de plume*. But as it is the name she chose for herself – and the one by which her Vine Press book would eventually be published – we shall call her Runia MacLeod.

Runia would go on to be Victor Neuburg's ultimate and most rewarding partner. In her, he found Kathleen's no-nonsense sensibility coupled with a fire for freedom and artistic expression – and, perhaps most indelibly, a staunch belief in his talents. In him, Runia found a man who, likewise, believed in her; a man who seemed to have little care or respect for traditional gender roles, and who saw her as an independent and equal thinker. Victor Neuburg and Runia MacLeod would spend the rest of his life together. They helped to found the Institute for the Scientific Treatment of Delinquency with the psychologist and surrealist Grace Pailthorpe as well as H.D. Jennings White. And, together, they created both the influential *Comment* magazine, and its social circle, sometimes called 'the Zoists', that acted as a kind of Bloomsbury group for outcasts.

Theirs was a genuine literary and personal relationship – they finally found *the right thing*, after years of trying (and failing) to *do the right thing*. As Arthur Calder-Marshall said of the couple, 'When, after protracted arguments between love and duty, the former had triumphed, it did not, as many fiery passions, burn itself to dust. It broke like a fine dawn over the Poet's life.'

When they met, the 'duty' part of their lives was still very much in charge, with both Victor and Runia still married to others. (In fact, they would remain so throughout their relationship.) But that was winding down.

In 1924, Kathleen gave birth to Victor B. Neuburg's only child, a son named Victor E. Neuburg but referred to as 'Toby' from childhood. Toby's arrival into the world did not exactly cement the bond between mother and father: within three months of his birth, Kathleen had begun a long-lasting affair. Vickybird's belief in sexual freedom was tested. It's a test he passed easily, going so far as to help Kathleen pack her bags and load the car for weekends away with her lover. Instead of getting angry, Victor moved on, spending increasing amounts of time at the Sanctuary.

For five years the couple remained together, he and Kathleen's relationship becoming something of a business deal, albeit with very little 'business' involved. There was Vickybird's allowance: a small amount for a single man, smaller still when it had to account for a wife and child, too. Then there was Vine Cottage, which Kathleen turned into an asset by providing bed and breakfast to paying guests. Sixty years later, Toby would recall a 'constant stream of visitors' in the later 1920s, likely sent by Neuburg's London contacts, including the likes of Tallulah Bankhead and Gertrude Stein.

Then there was The Vine Press, still trying everything to earn money – everything, that is, except publishing books that might sell. The Press was hard at work: in 1928, the singer Marian Anderson would spend weeks as a guest at Vine Cottage, and noted in her autobiography that Victor and Kathleen's primary occupation seemed to be cutting pages hot off the press. In the mid-1920s, following Toby's birth, the output from Vine Press leaned more towards Neuburg the 'publisher', rather than 'author'. He began working with London book-world mainstays P.J. (Percy) & A.E. (Arthur) Dobell to make and move his wares, and with projects well outside his 'normal' territory, he seems to have been trying what he could to expand his operation's viability. But visitors at the time noted the stacks of unsold Vine Press books, and years after the limited-edition *Lillygay* and *Songs of the Groves* books were produced, their author was still giving them away; still more were damaged in a flood at the Cottage in the mid-'20s.

Toby Neuburg, who would go on to be, among other things, a historian and bibliographer of small press books, points to this in his short, sweet memoir of his father:

> Because he was, in a business sense, hopelessly impractical and extremely generous, many of the Vine Press books were given away to friends … The result is that a Vine Press in fine condition not inscribed by Vickybird really is a scarce item! I can hear his laughter down the years…

Their pockets still thinly lined, the Neuburgs were, by the end of the 1920s, living almost entirely separate lives. Kathleen had her other relationship; Victor was traveling to London to see Runia regularly, even taking a young Calder-Marshall with him on one such journey. And much of the rest of his time, when he could, was spent at the Sanctuary and on his ever-increasing interest in politics. By the end of the decade it had become too much: the family moved to London, but not wholly together. They shared a legal address, but Victor's relationship with Runia was an open secret. He practically cohabitated with Runia, Charles Tharp and the couple's children for the first few years of the '30s, and when Runia moved to her own home in St John's Wood soon after, Neuburg became a fully-fledged resident.

With the departure from Steyning, The Vine Press came to its logical conclusion. It had served its purpose: it had saved Neuburg's life, and breathed a new one into many more. And it showed him his true calling: the gathering and inspiration of others.

After The Vine Press

Neuburg would go on to do his most historically significant work in the scant few years he had left. Always the protector, Hayter Preston got him a job as editor of the *Sunday Referee*'s Poet's Corner, through which Neuburg became briefly influential in British poetry. He discovered, and published, the first book by the soon-to-be very successful author Pamela Hansford Johnson. When poems arrived from a young Welshman, Dylan Thomas, they were so striking that some thought it might be a celebrated scribe playing a joke. Neuburg went on to publish several of Thomas's poems, and then the first book by the man who would become one of the 20th century's greatest English-language writers.

The majority of the Poet's Corner field was far from undiscovered geniuses, and much closer to The Vine Press. In his pages of the *Referee*, Neuburg sought to create a forum for discussion of poetry as much as anything – a community. When the *Sunday Referee* dissolved Poet's Corner after a couple of short years, he and Runia set out to fulfil that project with *Comment*, a weekly newsletter of poetry, politics and the arts that, in its 18-month run, was important to the arrival of surrealism in Britain and to the spreading of anti-fascist sentiment among the London art-and-literature world.

After moving into Runia's new home in St John's Wood, *Comment* spilled into real life with 'the Zoists'. This informal social circle included the likes of Thomas and Johnson, historian Brian Crozier, the surrealist artists Grace Pailthorpe and Reuben Mednikoff (who met through Neuburg) and old friend A.L. Morton. In some ways this circle was the culmination of Neuburg's life's work: a dendritic network that could replace what he'd missed from Crowley's circle, but without the sinister side.

Around this time, Rupert Croft-Cooke ran into Neuburg at a Chinese restaurant in London, coming out from a back-room meeting of socialists and anarchists. Back in the literary swim, living in London with Runia, away from Steyning and Kathleen, he was, as Croft-Cooke put it, 'writing and meeting young people. He had plans. His eyes in that long unchanged face were alight with enthusiasm.' In his diaries, Rold White saw it, too, commenting in 1931 that Vickybird in London seemed to be much improved in mental health, and reenergised. Like so many, White seems to have felt the need to save and protect Neuburg; to shield him as one might an innocent thing.

And yet, by 1937, Victor's life was over. At 54, and arguably doing his most important work, he began to succumb to illness – enough that *Comment* shuttered, with Victor unable to work and Runia dedicating herself to his care. He would struggle on for nearly three years, but in May of 1940, less than a month after his 57th birthday, he died of tuberculosis in Runia's home.

Legacy

Ostrobogulous. It's a word that Victor B. Neuburg summoned into being, and one that describes his life. Arthur Calder-Marshall used it frequently; it means, as he put it in his *Times Literary Supplement* review of Jean Overton Fuller's biography, 'the deep purple of bawdry of the finest dye', and he described Vickybird's etymological thinking: 'full of (Latin, *ulus*) rich (Greek, *ostro*) dirt (Schoolboy, *bog*).'

That the finest purple was draped over Victor Neuburg's life was entirely the doing of his Quixotic imagination. It was, ultimately, his greatest act of magick – to live a life that seemed to happen concurrent to, but not within, his own times. To live in such a manner is not a popular decision, even among other poets, as Dylan Thomas shows. In his biography of the Welshman, Andrew Lycett describes Neuburg, based on Thomas's letters as, 'an 1890s aesthete manqué'; Thomas himself didn't hold back so much in a letter of 1935:

> The Creature himself – I must tell you one day, if I haven't told you before, the story of how Aleister Crowley turned Vicky into a camel – is a nineteenth-century crank with mental gangrene, lousier than ever before, a product of a Jewish nuts-factory, an Oscar Tamed.

This, of the man who'd brought him to London and been his poetry's champion. Six months before this letter, Neuburg had wrangled money from the *Sunday Referee* to publish Thomas's first book, which set him on the path to stardom. But this was Neuburg's great downfall: he was a true believer in a world of cynics, and to too many people, that smacked of weakness.

That ever-buoyant belief in others is, however, Neuburg's legacy – and that of The Vine Press. He believed in 'the progressive thing', as Runia MacLeod put it: he believed that his work was, as he told Arthur Calder-Marshall, 'spreading the word'. The Vine Press wasn't merely a publisher of poetry, it was a battalion fighting in the ongoing war between beauty and philistinism, and Victor Neuburg was its Colonel.

In 1940, he died with his boots on, but the mantle was taken up by those he inspired: Jennings White, Croft-Cooke, Ethel Archer, Runia MacLeod – and, of course, Pamela Hansford Johnson, Dylan Thomas and Hayter Preston.

In 1947, MacLeod published what might be considered the final book of The Vine Press – her play, *Wax*. Toby Neuburg would later publish his own book under the imprint, in the 1960s, but *Wax* was almost certainly a long-discussed project, having been written in 1929. Regardless, both posthumous Vine Press books disappeared into the ether even more readily than their predecessors.

In the last months of Victor's life it is said he was contemplating a new book of poetry with his old friend, the legendary occult artist Austin Osman Spare. Days before his death, he referred the poet Vera Wainwright in his stead; in an alternate world, might the masks Spare drew for her have been illustrations for Neuburg? Might there have been a kind of return to magick, had he lived even one more year?

Hayter Preston told Jean Overton Fuller that Victor, 'gave up magic and spent the rest of his life feeling he was not doing what he was meant to be doing', which has become the dominant remembrance of Neuburg – that his post-Crowley life was an act of treading water. But that seems like a thorough misunderstanding of what Neuburg, and The Vine Press in particular, were meant to accomplish. To him, poetry *was* magick. It was a ritual. It was not the solitary action of the struggling writer at their desk, but an act of community.

Neuburg's ritual was to build those communities; his spells, the words that still linger on the pages of these books. Those spells don't all work. But some of them, some fair few lines that hover in the air when spoken – they conjure the vision of a different world; a world in which Victor Neuburg and his crew of outcasts won.

The following selections are taken from books
published by Victor B. Neuburg and The
Vine Press between 1920 and 1930, plus
one additional text published after
Neuburg's death. The texts are
faithful to the spirit of the
Vine Press originals, with
the exception of a very
few, and very minor,
typographical
corrections.

·/.

LILLYGAY:

AN ANTHOLOGY OF ANONYMOUS POEMS

Lillygay: An Anthology of Anonymous Poems
Victor B. Neuburg, editor-author (published anonymously).
Eric and Percy West, woodcut illustrations.
The Vine Press, Steyning. 1920.

The first book published by The Vine Press was arguably also its most 'successful'. *Lillygay* is a volume of anonymous verse – folksongs and tales, Scots ballads, a medieval song and a few thinly veiled Victor Neuburg originals. It speaks to Neuburg's re-immersion into poetry, eight years after *The Triumph of Pan* and his abandonment by the muse.

Those eight years must have seemed a lifetime. His love, Jeanne Heyse (aka Ione de Forest), had catalysed his eventual split from Aleister Crowley and, tragically young, taken her own life. Neuburg moved around: London, Hove, the West Country; a short, inglorious but life-changing stint at the Western Front and a convalescence in various army hospitals. He met Kathleen Rose Goddard, whom Vicky would eventually marry, and reacquainted himself with Hayter Preston. And by 1920 he and Preston – and, soon, Kathleen – were ensconced at Victor's Aunt Ti's property: Vine Cottage in Steyning.

But Aunt Ti didn't just give him her Downland bolthole. She provided him the capital and allowance that would help him acquire a hand-operated printing press and afford him the time to use it. There was, however, a stipulation, according to writer and friend Rupert Croft-Cooke: an agreement that led Neuburg to publish the work of others freely but his own work either anonymously or under a series of pseudonyms. Others posit that Neuburg published pseudonymously for personal reasons – blacklisted because of, or in hiding from, Crowley, or out of shame for his hidden role in Jeanne's suicide. This seems less likely, as Neuburg still wrote under his own name in other national publications (albeit infrequently). And, of course, there's simply the puckish Vickybird spirit – the man who constantly created his own words and linguistic affectations; the impish occult dramatist of Frater Omnia Vincam who admired poets such as Alcofribas Nasier (Rabelais), Bysshe Vanolis (James Thomson) and Æ (George William Russell).

With the new Vine Press, his partners Hayter Preston and Kathleen Rose, and new friends from around the corner, the Vickybird set to work printing the works that were inspiring him back into poetry. Jean Overton Fuller recalls him saying that when the muse returned, she spoke to him in the Scottish dialect, and that affection is reflected in *Lillygay*. The folksongs here are collected from 18th and 19th-century ballad books like *Ancient and Modern Scottish Songs, Heroic Ballads, etc.*, and *Ancient Poems, Ballads, and Songs of the Peasantry of England*. But amongst them are a few pieces adjusted, or perhaps written, by Neuburg: 'Lilly-white' and 'Rantum-tantum' are youthful songs praising poetry and lushness – almost fit for the playground, but also, of course, not. 'Sick Dick' is a rather outrageous portrait of the inebriated life. He is also, more obviously, responsible for the tops and tails (prologue, colophon) and the Epilogue – a slightly cleaned-up version of the First World War soldier's song 'No Balls at All', which he apparently sang around the house in its unexpurgated version.

Lillygay proved successful by Neuburg standards: five years later it was still being promoted as one of the best-reviewed and most popular Vine Press titles. This is probably due, in part, to two collaborators. First there were the Wests. Eric and Percy West were part of a long-standing Steyning family of publicans, agricultural labourers and, in the '20s, printers. Young men of around 23 and 21 respectively, Eric and Percy made the woodcuts that illustrate *Lillygay*; their older brother Dennis would soon make similar work for *Larkspur*. And, two years after its publication, the composer Peter Warlock would use *Lillygay* as the basis for a song cycle for voice and piano, including: 'The Distracted Maid', 'Johnnie wi' the Tye', 'The Shoemaker', 'Burd Ellen and Young Tamlane' and 'Rantum-tantum'. (Keith Anderson of Naxos Records has called Warlock's *Lillygay*, 'the best examples of English song-writing of the period.') Late in the 1920s, and near the end of his short life, Warlock would draw on *Lillygay* again, publishing 'Sick Dick' as part of an anthology he edited of writing about drink.

DEDICATION

TO POETS

I love my Sal: and her brave
    caresses;
I love the lullabie songs that She
    can croon;
Her lilly-white breasts, and her
    nut-brown tresses:
I could feed her lips on love with
    a wooden spoon.

PROLOGUE

Songs of ripe-lipped love and of honey-coloured laughter: old
    lamps for new: ancient lights.
Herein are little mirrors, but they are of the world;
tonguefuls of words, but new words of a new world, newly
coloured by the Angel of a new time. For a new Age is ever born
from the past. The Future alone is ancient upon the Spiral.
    The rainbow and the waterfall, the waving Tree and the
flaming Sword are one with Man, and these songs are songs of
his soul.

THE DISTRACTED MAID

One morning very early, one morning in
      the spring,
I heard a maid in Bedlam who
      mournfully did sing;
Her chains she rattled on her hands while sweetly
      thus sung she:
"I love my love, because I know my love loves
      me.

"Oh, cruel were his parents who sent my love to
      sea!
And cruel, cruel was the ship that bore my love
      from me;
Yet I love his parents, since they're his,
      although they've ruin'd me;
And I love my love, because I know my love
      loves me.

"Oh, should it please the pitying powers to call
      me to the sky,
I'd claim a guardian angel's charge around my
      love to fly;
To guard him from all dangers how happy should
      I be!
For I love my love, because I know my love loves
      me.

"I'll make a strawy garland, I'll make it wondrous
      fine,
With roses, lilies, daisies I'll mix the eglantine;
And I'll present it to my love when he returns
      from sea;

For I love my love, because I know my love loves
   me.

"Oh, If I were a little bird to build upon his
   breast!
Or if I were a nightingale to sing my love to
   rest!
To gaze upon his lovely eyes all my reward
   should be;
For I love my love, because I know my love loves
   me.

"Oh, If I were an eagle to soar into the sky!
I'd gaze around with piercing eyes where I my
   love might spy;
But ah! unhappy maiden, that love you ne'er
   shall see:
Yet I love my love, because I know my love loves
   me."

ELORÉ LO

In a garden so green of a May morning,
Heard I my lady pleen of paramours;
Said she, "My love so sweet, come ye not yet, not yet,
Hight you not me to meet amongst the flowers?
Eloré! Eloré! Eloré! Eloré!
I love my lusty love, Eloré lo!

"The light upspringeth, the dew down dingeth,
The sweet lark singeth her hours of prime;
Phoebus up spenteth, joy to rest wenteth,
So lost is mine intents, and gone is the time.
Eloré! Eloré! Eloré! Eloré!
I love my lusty love, Eloré lo!

"Danger my dead is, false fortune my feid is,
And languor my lead is, but hope I despair,
Disdain my desire is, so strangeness my fear is,
Deceit out of all ware; adieu, I fare.
Eloré! Eloré! Eloré! Eloré!
I love my lusty love, Eloré lo!"

Then to my lady blyth did I my presence kyth,
Saying, "My bird, be glad! am I not yours?"
So in my arms too did I the lusty jo,
And kissed her times mo than night hath hours.
Eloré! Eloré! Eloré! Eloré!
I love my lusty love, Eloré lo!

"Live in hope, lady fair, and repel all despair,
Trust that your true love shall you not betray;
When deceit and langour is banisht from your bower,
I'll be your paramour and shall you please;
Eloré! Eloré! Eloré! Eloré!
I love my lusty love, Eloré lo!

"Favour and duty unto your bright beauty;
Confirmed has lawtie obeyed to truth;
So that your soverance, heartilie but variance,
Mark in your memorance mercy and ruth.
Eloré! Eloré! Eloré! Eloré!
I love my lusty love, Eloré lo!

"Yet for your courtesie banish all jealousie;
Love for love lustily, do me restore;
Then with us lovers young true love shall rest and
    reign,
Solace shall sweetly sing for ever more;
Eloré! Eloré! Eloré! Eloré!
I love my lusty love, Eloré lo!"

BONFIRE SONG

The bonny month of June is crowned
    With the sweet scarlet rose;
    Each grove and meadow all around
    With lovely pleasure flows.

And I walked out to yonder green
    One evening so fair,
All where the fair maids might be seen
    Playing at the bonfire.

Hail! lovely nymphs, be not too coy,
    But freely yield your charms;
Let love inspire with mirth and joy
    In Cupid's lovely arms.

Bright Luna spread her light around
    The gallants for to cheer,
As they lay sporting on the ground
    At the fair June bonfire.

All on the pleasant dewy mead
      They shared each other's charms,
Till Phoebus' beams began to spread,
      And coming day alarms.

Whilst larks and linnets sing so sweet
      To cheer each lovely swain,
Let each prove true unto their love,
      And so farewell the plain.

BURD ELLEN AND YOUNG TAMLANE

B urd Ellen sits in her bower windowe,
      With a double laddy double, and for the double dow,
Twisting the red silk and the blue,
      With the double rose and the May-hay.

And whiles she twisted, and whiles she twam,
      With a double laddy double, and for the double dow,
And whiles the tears fell down amang,
      With the double rose and the May-hay.

Till once there cam' by Young Tamlane,
      With a double laddy double, and for the double dow,
"Come light, oh light, and rock your young son!"
      With the double rose and the May-hay.

"If ye winna rock him, ye may let him rair,
      "With a double laddy double, and for the double dow,
"For I ha'e rockit my share and mair !
      "With the double rose and the May-hay."

Young Tamlane to the seas he's gane,
    With a double laddy double, and for the double dow,
And a' women's curse in his company's gane!
    With the double rose and the May-hay.

LILLY-WHITE

Lilly-white her hands are,
    Lilly-white her thighs,
Little Starry strands are
    The locks above her eyes.

Violets her eyes are,
    Her hands are valley-lillies,
Her eyes are like the skies are,
    Her breasts are daffodillies.

Violet and lilly-gold,
    Petalled daffodills,
She's joyous as the hilly gold
    Upon the Gorsy Hills.

I'll pluck her valley-lillies,
    And steal her violets,
I'll turn her daffodillies
    To gold-lipped triolets.

I'll cross the hills beyond; oh !
    I'll seek her in the sun;
I'll sing to her my rondeau
    Until her heart is won.

And oh! her hands are lillies,
    And lilly-white her thighs,
But still her softest thrill is
    Beneath her violet eyes.

SICK DICK;
OR, THE DRUNKARD'S TRAGEDY

Dick was sick last night, good lack!
    With a colley-walley-walley-walley-
        walley-walley-wabbles;
    He walked to the Lion, but they carried him back,
    And Dick was sick all over the cobbles.

He walked to the Lion as lordly as a lecher,
    With a colley-walley-walley-walley-
        walley-walley-wabbles;
But they bore him back on a home-made stretcher,
    And Dick was sick all over the cobbles.

He swilled and swallowed like some old sow,
    With a colley-walley-walley-walley-
        walley-walley-wabbles;
Till he belched and bellowed like our milch-cow,
    And Dick was sick all over the cobbles.

The ale at the Lion is bright and old,
    With a colley-walley-walley-walley-
        walley-walley-wabbles;
And that's what made Dick overbold,
    And Dick was sick all over the cobbles.

Dick grew loving as it grew late,
    With a colley-walley-walley-walley-
        walley-walley-wabbles;
And he gave a hug to Slommicky Kate,
    And Dick was sick all over the cobbles.

But when he tried to kiss Jane Trollop,
    With a colley-walley-walley-walley-
        walley-walley-wabbles;
He went to the floor with a whack and a wallop,
    And Dick was sick all over the cobbles.

For he bussed Jane Trollop bang in the eye,
    With a colley-walley-walley-walley-
        walley-walley-wabbles;
While her Cullie Claude was standing by,
    And Dick was sick all over the cobbles.

And Cullie Claude is a surly swain,
    With a colley-walley-walley-walley-
        walley-walley-wabbles;
For when Dick got up he downed him again,
    And Dick was sick all over the cobbles.

So we set Dick up upon a chair,
    With a colley-walley-walley-walley-
        walley-walley-wabbles;
And wiped the saw-dust from his hair,
    And Dick was sick all over the cobbles.

And he's better today, and says, Good Lack,
    With a colley-walley-walley-walley-
        walley-walley-wabbles;
Take me on a stretcher and I'll walk back,
    And Dick was sick all over the cobbles.

A LYKE-WAKE DIRGE

This ae nighte, this ae nighte,
　　　　Everie nighte and alle,
Fire, and sleete, and candle-lighte,
　　　　And Christe receive thy saule.

When thou from hence away art past,
　　　　Everie nighte and alle,
To Whinnie-muir thou comest at last,
　　　　And Christe receive thy saule.

If ever thou gavest hosen and shoon,
　　　　Everie nighte and alle,
Sit thee down and put them on,
　　　　And Christe receive thy saule.

If hosen and sham thou gavest nane,
　　　　Everie nighte and alle,
The whinnes shall pricke thee to the bare bane,
　　　　And Christe receive thy saule.

From Whinnie-muir when thou mayst passe,
　　　　Everie nighte and alle,
To Brigg o' Dread thou comest at last,
　　　　And Christe receive thy saule.

From Brigg o' Dread when thou mayst passe,
　　　　Everie nighte and alle,
To Purgatory Fire thou comest at last,
　　　　And Christe receive thy saule.

If ever thou gavest meate or drinke,
      Everie nighte and alle,
The fire shall never make thee shrinke,
      And Christe receive thy saule.

If meate or drinke thou gavest nane,
      Everie nighte and alle,
The fire will burn thee to the bare bane,
      And Christe receive thy saule.

This ae nighte, this ae nighte,
      Everie nighte and alle,
Fire, and sleete, and candle-lighte,
      And Christe receive thy saule.

JOHNNIE WI' THE TYE

Johnnie cam' to our toun,
    To our toun, to our toun,
Johnnie cam' to our toun,
The body wi' the tye;
And O as he kittl'd me,
Kittl'd me, kittl'd me,
O as he kittl'd me –
But I forgot to cry.

He gaed thro' the fields wi' me,
The fields wi' me, the fields wi' me,
He gaed thro' the fields wi' me,
And doun amang the rye;
Then O as he kittl'd me,
Kittl'd me, kittl'd me,
Then O as he kittl'd me –
But I forgot to cry.

THE SHOEMAKER

S hoemaker, shoemaker, are ye within?
   A fal a falladdie fallee;
 Hae ye got shoes to fit me so trim,
  For a kiss in the morning early?

O fair may, come in and see,
   A fal a falladdie fallee,
I've got but ae pair and I'll gi'e them to thee
  For a kiss in the morning early.

He's ta'en her in behind the bench,
   A fal a falladdie fallee,
And there he has fitted his own pretty wench
   With a kiss in the morning early.

When twenty weeks war come and gane,
   A fal a falladdie fallee,
The maid cam' back to her shoemaker then,
  For a kiss in the morning early.

Oh, says she, I can't spin at a wheel,
   A fal a falladdie fallee,
If ye can't spin at a wheel, ye may spin at a rock,
For I go not to slight my own pretty work
   That was done in the morning early.

When twenty weeks war come and gone,
   A fal a falladdie fallee,
The maid she brought forth a braw young son,
   For her kiss in the morning early.

Oh, says her father, we'll cast it out,
      A fal a falladdie fallee,
It is but the shoemaker's dirty clout,
      It was got in the morning early.

Oh, says her mother, we'll keep it in,
      A fal a falladdie fallee,
It was born a prince, and it may be a king,
      It was got in the morning early.

When other maids gang to the ball,
      A fal a falladdie fallee,
She must sit and dandle her shoemaker's awl,
      For her kiss in the morning early.

When other maids gang to their tea,
      A fal a falladdie fallee,
She must sit at hame and sing balillalee,
      For her kiss in the morning early.

RANTUM-TANTUM

Who'll play at Rantum-tantum
      Over the fields in May?
Oh, maidens fair, 'Od grant 'em
      Rantum-tantum play!

The dawning fields are rimy,
      White in the sun-rise way,
But oh! the fields smell thymy
      Later in the day!

And oh! may the fields be pearly
    With dawn and virgin dew,
And may my love come early!
    And may my love be true!

Oh, the fields are green in day-time,
    And the trees are white in May,
And Rantum-tantum May-time
    's the time for lovers' play.

The little fern-fronds are curly,
    And the apple-boughs are white,
And the steers are brown and burly,
    And the birds sing for delight.

Oh, hey for Rantum-tantum!
    Come out, my love, to see:
And for virgins, Oh, 'Od grant 'em
    What virgins grant to me !

EPILOGUE

Now all you young poets,
    come listen awhile:
I'll sing you a song that will make you
    all smile;
It's about a young lady so fair and so tall
Who married a man who had no heart
    at all!
    No heart at all!
    No heart at all!
    How could he love her with no
    heart at all?

Now on the first evening, ere they had
        retired,
She thought she would see if her love
        was desired,
She sought for his passion – his passion
        was small;
She sought for his heart – he had no
        heart at all!
        No heart at all!
        No heart at all!
        How could he love her with no
        heart at all?

Dear daughter, dear daughter, oh, don't
        look so sad,
But treat him the same as I treated your
        dad:
There's many a man will be willing to
        call
And make love for the man who has no
        heart at all!
        No heart at all!
        No heart at all!
        Zounds to the man who has no
        heart at all!

COLOPHON

Pale lilies throned in silver jars,
        White stars in red-gold skies,
Slim olivine wild nenuphars
        Blowing broad melodies.

Grey horses in the hippodrome
        Of wheeling stars; symposia
Of Hybla-scented honeycomb,
        Violet-breathed ambrosia.

Or what you care, or what you will,
        Or what you dare; 'tis one:
Take every dewy daffodil
        Of Art and Song and Sun.

Take what you will, and thrill and thrill
        As thrill the windy skies;
Guide the soul-steeds with skill, with skill:
        Rede well these harmonies.

GABRIELE D'ANNUNZIO'S APPEAL TO EUROPE

Gabriele d'Annunzio's Appeal to Europe
Hayter Preston, translator.
Broadsheet Number One.
The Vine Press, London & Steyning. 1920.

In 1920, Vine Press printed its 'Broadsheet Number One', a poem translated from the Italian by Neuburg's lifelong friend William Edward Hayter Preston (usually referred to simply by his surnames). The choice seems bizarre: Gabriele D'Annunzio, the Italian nationalist poet, politician and soldier, and his poem from October, 1918 – 'The Prayer of Sernaglia'. Better known from its key phrase, 'Vittoria Nostra, Non Sarai Mutilata' – origin of the concept of the 'mutilated victory' – the Prayer would become a rhetorical cornerstone of Italy's fascist movement. At the other end of the political spectrum, Preston and Neuburg would each go on to be closely allied with leftist and anarchist movements, and directly involved with anti-fascism in 1920s and '30s England. (Hayter Preston would eventually be villainised by his fellow leftists in the mid-'30s for demanding that all political objectives be put on hold, all rivalries dropped, until fascism was defeated across Europe.)

So, why this? D'Annunzio would've been well known to the two men. His decadent turn-of-the-century poetry, and in particular the volume *Halcyon*, would certainly have featured in both men's libraries; his Romantic attachment to the 'adventurer-poet' particularly appealing. His work was a flag to the Soho scene from which they came: in her memoir, *Laughing Torso*, Nina Hamnett puts reading D'Annunzio in a line of Soho Bohemian musts, alongside seeing Sarah Bernhardt and trying 'to feel fatal'. The Italian was also a favourite of the American ex-pat modernist Ezra Pound, who would go on to have an unsavoury relationship with Italian fascism in general. Preston and Neuburg both knew Pound. A 1920s edgelord to be sure, Pound flitted around the edges of the Crowley circle in the years before the First World War. He had an admiration for (more likely: 'affair with') Jeanne Heyse, to whom he dedicated two poems, one in her lifetime and one inspired by her demise. Preston edited

Pound for the sole issue of *The Cerebralist*, and flirted with the ideas of masculinity contained within both that philosophy and the macho work of D'Annunzio. As you'd imagine, Aleister Crowley and D'Annunzio were acquainted: it seems impossible that Neuburg wouldn't have known the Italian's poetry.

Two things about 'The Appeal' seem certain. Firstly, its translator and printer found the language intoxicating. The flourish of its rhetoric; the poem's Romantic grandiosity; the pomposity of its religious iconography – it is a fascinating turn of phrase, even in Preston's relatively clunky translation, relying on linguistic anachronisms as Neuburg would do throughout his own translations and reprintings. (Take the most famous, penultimate line: in Preston, 'Victory, thou shalt not be mutilated / No one can break thy knees or clip thy feathers.' Other translators give it modern flow: 'Our Victory, you will not be mutilated / No one can shatter your kneecaps or clip your wings.') D'Annunzio's 'favourite vehicles for images', as one contemporary called them, would've been inspirational to The Vine Press: angelic language that also contains the foul and the putrid; blood and vomit. The underlying 'appeal' to the nascent Vine Press may well have been in the poem's less-political message: that there are victors who are losers, and losers who win. That the real victory can be made only in the telling of the tale.

Secondly, it's certain that both men would come to regret its publication. As a test of the new Vine Press font, a setting of its style, and an imagining of broadsheet possibilities it seems successful enough. But the broadsheet itself never made it very far, and they were likely glad for it as the '20s moved on and Italy – and its rhetoric – descended into something abhorrent. The piece isn't mentioned again.

GABRIELE D'ANNUNZIO'S
Appeal to Europe

Translated by HAYTER PRESTON

Vittoria Nostra, Non Sarai Mutilata

Victory, thou shalt not be mutilated

¶ V.

51. O sudden season of rapture which art neither spring nor autumn, but art that where the eternal laurel yields its fruits!

52. O swift spirit which re-fertilizeth earth's sores, and from the distress of destroyed fields causeth a shiver to run thro' the future harvest!

53. O rivers recrossed, swelling with joy, like veins which bring pride to the heart of the Country, and a blush to its brow!

54. O unencumbered valleys now breathing sweetness so pure that the dead seem to sleep here in the arms of Mary as did her Son!

55. O sovereign songs, most holy among the holiest hymns, voiced by the agony of the oppressed who hear the approaching steps of their liberators!

56. O bands, O thorns, O scourges, abjuring and shame, burden and yoke, thirst and hunger, sanies and blood, O passion of Christ and of the world, O victory beyond death!

57. Who shall change this grandeur and this impetuous beauty in a long argument of old folk, in a decrepit counsel of deceits?

58. Scribes' ink for martyrs' blood? The martyrdom of years bought with a packet of deducted papers?

59. If the mutilator kneel, if he raise his filthy hands, if he cast down his contrite snout, sever his thumbs or wrists, break his tusks and jaws.

60. Stamp upon him the red-hot mark between brow and brow, between shoulder and shoulder. And this would not suffice. Such a race if dissolved by fear revives again from its husk.

61. And pass along. The dead are preceding you. To the dead, the buried and the unburied, the heel-bone has remained to tread upon the foreign soil.

62. What was said in God repeateth itself: "For the souls of those creatures who have been afflicted with spasms at every corner of the road; and had no hands to cross in their prayer."

63. Victory, thou shalt not be mutilated. No one can break thy knees or clip thy feathers. Where runnest thou? Where fliest thou?

64. Thy course is beyond night. Thy flight is beyond dawn. What was said in God repeateth itself: "The skies are less wide than thy wings."

SWIFT WINGS:

SONGS IN SUSSEX

Swift Wings: Songs in Sussex
(Published anonymously.)
Victor B. Neuburg, author.
Beatrice Linda Stanbrough, cover design.
The Vine Press, Steyning. 1921.

The towns and villages sprinkled around the escarpment of the South Downs are always 'nestled'. They are often 'chocolate-box-y', frequently 'idyllic', almost always 'quiet' or 'rustling'; I have seen many in which 'it's as though time has stood still'. Steyning, where Victor B. Neuburg lived and operated The Vine Press, was all of these things in the 1920s and is, still, today.

And yet it's not: while Steyning, nine miles northwest of central Brighton, is indeed nestled among the pastoral idyll of the South Downs, it is also busy for a small country market town, and boasts a relatively sizable population. Steyning sits where the River Adur cuts through the South Downs – a line of hills running parallel to the sea along England's southeastern coast that has acted as the region's backbone and arterial pathway for millennia. As such, Steyning has been a stopping point, market destination and important crossroads for centuries. It is so today, and it was in the 1920s: Rupert Croft-Cooke writes in his autobiographical volume *Glittering Pastures* that by the mid-'20s, Neuburg kept the front windows to Vine Cottage tightly shut in an effort to keep out the noise of automobiles. But those first months of life in the country, after a life of London – this move to Camelot with his new round table – were always going to be 'Arthurian … Lemurian … reverberant, thrasonical' for the Vickybird. It is in this rapturous Romantic moment that Neuburg anonymously published his poems of Sussex as *Swift Wings*.

After *Lillygay's* publication, Neuburg exploded into a spell of prolific walking and writing. His new home, beside the Downs and at the foot of the (genuinely) ancient, mysterious and compelling Chanctonbury Ring, became a new source of inspiration. But so did more familiar grounds around Brighton and Hove and vicinities, which seem to have suddenly revealed themselves to Vickybird as sites of refuge from the modern. The poet joined his interests – for magick, sensuality, folk culture, Romanticism and, with his new work, landscape – into a passion for the mystical experience of place that we might well recognise in the 21st century.

Most of the poems in *The Triumph of Pan* had been dedicated by name to people with whom Neuburg had important (if not always positive) relationships: the original 'class' of Crowley's order the A∴A∴; the women he admired and pursued; his family, both blood and literary. In *Swift Wings*, essentially his next published book of original poems, the same could be said for these important – often beloved; occasionally feared – icons of the Sussex Downland landscape. But the book in its whole is dedicated to KAROG, a typically Neuburgian acronym for Kathleen Rose Goddard (soon-to-be Neuburg) – and it is in this moment that his relationship with Kathleen must have reached its apex. Her presence is as strong as the landscape's, and only slightly more subtly drawn.

I have added brief notes on a few of the places that are the subject of Swift Wings' *poems.*

DEDICATION

TO KAROG

L ithe shall be your lover;
        Blithe shall be your breast;
How your heart shall hover
        When your breast is prest!

Be green trees above you;
        The blue sea beyond;
Make your lover love you
        If you'd have him fond.

So he still shall follow,
        Your siren-glamoured man:
Be yours the wise Apollo,
        Be his the lurking Pan.

PUBLISHERS' NOTE

T he Poems in this Volume have been selected–at the
Author's Suggestion–from the much larger Work,
"Starcraft", which is to Appear this Autumn from The Vine Press.

PROLOGUE

Songs of the South land,
            Songs of sward and sea,
Wrought by a crafty hand
            To an old melody.

All my songs were heard before,
            All my words were sung,
Here beside a Southern shore,
            But in an alien tongue.

Perfect from the Portal,
            Towering from the Tomb,
Sounds the Song Immortal
            In sempiternal bloom.

Behind lies the sunlight,
            Before lies the day;
Lo! there is but one Light,
            One only Way.

One Way is certain:
            Oh, my Southern shore!
There is light behind the curtain;
            That and nothing more.

CUCKFIELD

Set in the key of blue, with harmonies
  Bee-brown, is Cuckfield, land of green and dew,
With hanging woods and opulent chestnut-trees
  Set in the key of blue

When Sussex' downs were leafier, and more new
  The wonders of the woodlands and the seas,
This lowland love was "Field of the Cuckoo."

Then some new Poet, seeking images
  For towns, heard Cuckoo-calls, and christened you
The Cuckoo Field, land of gold melodies
  Set in the key of blue.

SHOREHAM HILLS

Up on the hills, in the sun's risen calories,
  There is a winding way;
There the wind blows in harmonies of Malory's,
  There Arthur still has sway;
Shoreham lies under the great green galleries
  Of the great golden Day.

And it is England still; the old Arthurian
  History flames forth in gold;
There errant knight is mingled with centurion,
  And all is bright and bold;
All the world's back to the lost Lemurian
  Age on the wind-swept wold.

And it is Day, reverberant, thrasonical;
    Here is the ancient quorum
Of far old races; here's the brave old chronicle,
    Celts, Britons, Romans, in the forum;
The old brave gods, eternal and ironical,
    Look over the heights of Shoreham.

Shoreham-by-Sea is Steyning's larger neighbour at the mouth of the Adur. The town itself is pre-Roman, and its surrounding hills (particularly west, towards Worthing) were economically busy at least as early as the Neolithic.

OLD STEYNE

It is divine, an emerald light
Set in the sombre breast of night:
A wavering nocturne in a town,
With silver starlight looking down
Upon the breeze-tossed, dark green trees
Murmuring soft night-harmonies.

A symphony of duskiness,
A rustling world of foliaged stress;
The cars glide by on living wires,
Windows smile down with human fires
Within them. Did Beethoven dream
A lovelier light, a tenderer gleam,
A subtler green, a softer breath
Than this Old Steyne, that witnesseth
Beauty set in a living crown,
An artist-heart in a throbbing town?

Keats and Corot would never make
A fairer world for Beauty's sake;
Turner's dream of amethyst,
Written down in a golden mist
By the feathery pencil of Paul Verlaine,
Would never achieve the strange chance gain
Of this delight of utter green,
This shadowy wonder called Old Steyne.

The Old Steyne (or Steine) is a central avenue in Brighton, once gridded with tram lines.

RICHARD JEFFRIES

A hapless Greek, loathing Art's usurpature
   Of beauty in the world; who loved the lure
   Of fields and hills and seas, with eyes too pure
To bear our hideous mask, flat in inflature
Of folly and filth. His was the candidature
      For the old life, when the world's heart beat sure
      Against the sunny sky, in the mature
Worship of Beauty, soul and veil of Nature.

Bitter our world was to him, who loved still
The Golden World of eld, the mystic Hill
      Of Olympus, navel of the Ægean Sea.
What was his portion in our baser part?
Death. And what slew him? This: he broke his heart
      Against the eternal rock of Ecstasy.

The famed Victorian nature writer lived his final years in West Sussex.

A RIVER-BED

The belt of sea-board town's skin-deep; a single-mile inland
The strange, eternal, green downs stand: where once a river ran
There's a green road untrod of man, and on that secret way
The hovering elementals play over the sunken sand.

The rocks are garbed in sunny green, the sea is still their lover;
White butterflies delirious hover: where once the Ouse full-flowed
The busy lizard's made a road; where once the barbel swam,
The little, simple, crying lamb finds fossils in the clover.

The sea's spell lingers, loiters still; ever it shall remain:
A faithful lover is the main, though never to his bed
He may return to lay his head: a peace surpassing peace
Broods dreaming in this world-release, this land of utter gain.

And often on a sunny noon mist-beings hold their hallows
Over the docks and mallows, over the sunken sea,
Relics of Pagan empery, before the Celtic reign,
Hold here their mysteries again in ancient grass-girt shallows.

There is no shade at all; the earth cracks in the summer-swoon;
Only the shadowy rocks are strewn upon the parching land;
The green-girt vestiges of sand lie boiling in the blaze.
The old sea-empire now is Day's, the mystery of Noon.

OVINGDEAN

Upon the hills are infinite shades of green,
  Nuance eternal in the shifting light;
  Clouds on the cliffs; the subtlety of night;
The supreme sun; the moon, cool, calm, serene,
Forever young, things that have ever been;
    Forever old, in the earth-legend's might,
    Lifting and drifting: cloudy, coloured, bright,
Over the hills of valleyed Ovingdean.

Who would not win the passion of the pencil?
  The gifted glory of the living line?
Who would not steal the sternness of the stencil,
  The canvas-call that slays the Philistine?
To mould the stone to everlasting life?
To make a tree eternal with a knife?

Ovingdean is a small village east of Brighton.

HOVE STREET

Still the old airs! Vainly the fools 'improve'!
  Thought lingers solidly; a lasting stain
  Of thought, of dream, of love, of hate, of pain.
After the centuries there is a grove
Of oaks here still; white, furious figures move
    Stormily to an old tempestuous strain;
    Red drips remain where once were votives slain
In the centuries before the birth of Hove.

The impression stays, violet, violent, vivid;
    A rush of red; a crushing crimson relic;
        A scarlet stain, flushing the astral fluid
With purple, and the heart of it is livid.
    What priestly prayer, what aureole Angelic
        Can slay the splendid spells of the dark Druid?

WHITE HAWK HILL

You shed no shadow, O my sensitive
  Divine delight of life, whereby I live.
Yet are you of the earth, for earth's a star:
And only stars give birth to what you are;
The very gods conceive the thing you give.

O diamond-dust, soul of a hell-dark sign!
O Child Immortal of a mortal line!
The sight that sees the Night within the night;
The sight that sees the Light within the light;
Doth this gift not suffice? This gift is mine!

'Whether in Naishapur or Babylon',
Or upon White Hawk Hill, the tale is one;
But oh! my scented seaboard, how I love you;
The gorse behind you, and the sky above you,
And overhead the same eternal Sun!

The setting changes; and the figures change;
Through sunken islands and lost lands I range;
Still to return to the old loved illusion;
And still the light shines through the fierce confusion,
The same as ever, always fresh and strange.

Centuries pass; the drowned man knows the sea
His mother; and the buried man is free
To worship Earth; he who hath passed through fire
Knows utterly the Sun for source and sire;
Hence love I all the earth, as earth loves me.

We who are burned by fire, buried in earth,
Drowned in the water, know the secret mirth
Sung to the stars by wandering elementals;
The Soul of all things; the true transcendentals
Deeper than death, above the need of birth.

We who have passed into the Upper Air
Thence behold Earth, and know how she is fair.
More than her sister Stars sweet Earth doth love us;
She holds our hearts: the stars are high above us.
O Mother Earth! Stars are too far and rare!

O White Hawk Hill, above you shines the moon;
O White Hawk Hill, the early stars are strewn
About you. O my Mother, Mother Earth;
I praise the gods who gave me here my birth,
Birth and rebirth that ends in trancèd swoon.

I shall return from ecstasy to you,
While among stars you swim; while still the blue
Illusion holds you in the abyss of fire;
I shall return to satiate my desire;
To feel the green earth-kiss, eternal, true.

I shall return; the Green Star has me still,
Brain, body, soul and heart. My spirit's will
From trancèd sleep of splendour will be drawn
Back to the Green Star of the Golden Dawn:
I shall return; even to White Hawk Hill.

Whitehawk Camp is an important prehistoric site located in Brighton.

WILLIAM COLLINS

Solid in old red brick that breathes the Georges,
Redolent of port and beefsteak orgies,
Is somnolent and Tory Chichester;
For this I love her dullness: that in her
Was born the Poet, who was born to sing
The perfect lyric of the Evening.

But the poor Poet loathed his father's mart,
And went to London, where he broke his heart;
Broken and young and beautiful he died;
Chatterton, Otway, Keats, some few beside
Died so, but happy Collins lived to sing
The perfect Song sung to the Evening.

Exquisite Evening so worshipped him,
She dwelt with him until his mind grew dim;
He had drunken of her wine, and he was laid,
Unknown, unsung, beneath her dusky shade.
One perfect Song her lover sang to her,
Her hapless Poet born in Chichester.

Little young Collins sang, but once he knew
The joyous taste of pure Castalian dew.
In Chichester was born one perfect rose,
And in all love, a brother Poet goes,
A pilgrim, to the staid old Tory shrine,
For one pale rose, one draught of perfect wine.

The mad poet Collins began and ended his life in the city of Chichester, southwest of Steyning.

OCTOBER

In gardens of grey the springs are in spate,
　　Flowers are fallen and leaves whirled away.
Night-fall is early, and dawning is late,
　　In gardens of grey.

Ocean's in flood and the air's strong with spray;
　　Starless and sombre, the earth's big with fate,
Waters and winds are the lords of the day.

Wild are the waves under skies of cold slate,
　　The mountains are veiled and the wild horses neigh:
Colossal it looms, October's huge freight,
　　In gardens of grey.

ROTTINGDEAN

When the spray-tingling air was soft and thin
　　About the enchanted sea-board,
The silver splendour of a violin
　　Made the starred sky a key-board.

Where sapphire cliffs rival the opal sea,
　　While Naiads sing between
Opal and sapphire in an emerald key,
　　There, there was Rottingdean.

The Southern land vibrated; the white string
　　Tingled to white desire;
And Sappho strode the shore, a living thing,
　　With a huge golden lyre.

O gold and green, O living green and gold,
O word in gold and green!
Why does all Hellas suddenly unfold
In radiant Rottingdean?

Rottingdean is one of many villages east of Brighton, between the Downs and the sea. Its windmill is iconic, potentially one model for Swift Wings' cover illustration.

FULKING HILL

G rey, level eyes sweep round the laughing valley,
   Immortal in their sure, intense mortality;
   Transcendent in austerest, fierce morality
Of artist-love. Rooks make their noisy sally;
The wind-wheat song floats up in a swift rally
   Of Nature's perfect master-tones, legality
   Of all the lyres of man. Here is sodality
Of Art. Here form, light, sound blend naturally.

Poppies, white-drifting clouds, the red geranium,
   The undulating, solid sea of hills,
      The invisible lark, still shouting at the azure;
Was it not so in Tyre and Herculaneum,
   My mortal Artist of immortal thrills,
      Watching and dumb from
         Fulking Hill's embrasure?

Fulking Hill, north of Brighton, overlooks the great valley of Devil's Dyke.

FRENCHLANDS

Here the world's yellow. Here the cosmic yolk
Broke on the Star, and here these flowers awoke;
This is the single soul that hath no fellow
For secret light. Here the whole world is yellow.

Suns immature are yellow thus, but mellow
They turn to summer gold; therefore the yellow
Is spring-dawn, youth-tide, green-born-gold, awake
Before the Summer, for a promise' sake.

Here the embrazured sunlight sets awake
Soft yellow light, for unborn Summer's sake.
Here a whole world awaits the wakened Will
Promised by primrose, dreamed from daffodil.

Here the whole world soft-throbs into the thrill
That shall be born as yellow daffodil.
Here the world's yellow, where spring-light awoke
The golden gleaming of the yellow yolk.

This is the heart that throbs within the hill!
This is the Word that waits upon the Will!
This is the flood that shall all life fulfil!
That is the promise of the daffodil!

A 16th-century farmhouse outside of Steyning.

THE SEA IN MOONLIGHT

Syrened by song, molten by melody,
　　The wondering heart delays, and inly dies,
　　Drawn to deep death by midnight harmonies:
Chords that crash softly in a silver key.
What word can rival this one note, set free
　　From a light shore where new-born stars arise,
　　Where rocks are charmed by silver Naiad-eyes
That watch the moon-dawn on the restless sea?

Light is not light; it is the secret scent
　　Of moonlit air: sound is not sound; it is
　　The sense of silver in these mysteries
Of midnight orchestration; dream-veils rent
　　By the white lightning-flash of Diana's bow
　　Shot from her shore in flames of scarlet snow.

NIGHT-PIECE

The dusky frame of Night encloses
　　The palimpsest of day;
Tomorrow, tomorrow the birth of roses,
　　Tonight the sombre way.

Away and away in the sombre frame,
　　Hidden deeply, the light
Lies secure, the nameless Flame
　　Informing the heart of Night.

O Night, O Night of the dusky brow,
   Night of the luminous eyes,
Your heart is the home of the live, light Now;
   Your song is a world-uprise!

Wind on wild waters! Dreams in the dusk!
   Bud-stars under the snow!
Grey and chill are amber and musk,
   But the red heart cries below!

EX CATHEDRA

O ver the close-ranked forest pines
   The dark sky and the moon;
Is straight-compacted, silent lines
   Beneath night's flowering noon.
The hour of cloud and grey and moth –
Taciturn heaven of the Goth.

A poet came who dreamed in stone
   A mediæval dream
Of monks who sought the Light alone,
   Hermits who found the Gleam;
The sombre age's lonely light
Informed the artist-eremite.

And Ypres and Chartres saw Notre Dame
   Born of the lonely mood;
When night was still and dark and calm
   Craftsmen in stone and wood
Found golden, mystic images
And filigreed, strange traceries.

Out of the dark the living Light;
 The moon within the pool;
Here the dark poet came at night,
 Sombre and true and cool,
To home of shadow-play and moth,
The living temple of the Goth.

COOMBES

L ost in the hills where dock with nettle blooms,
 And the sheep feed,
Lies little, haunted, old, forgotten Coombes,
 A secret Church indeed.

Habitants gone and houses fallen away,
 It lies lost, lone,
The tiny Church, its atmosphere decay,
 A dying human stone.

Yet – when man goes, the secret things come back,
 Old Pagan things;
And there is old life in the ruined track,
 Strange feet, and stranger wings.

And when you linger near at evening,
 In the grey mood,
Strange breezes flutter, and strange voices sing,
 An eerie multitude.

For sprites are undisturbed in the last light,
 And on the level
Old mossy churchyard, just before the night,
 They hold unholy revel.

Then I get home. I hate a place of haunt
    That is not peace:
It is too much; indecently they flaunt,
    The spirits, their release.

Some seem for their Return too much decayed;
    They've stayed to lurch,
Poor Christian sprites, too long; too long they've played
    About the haunted Church.

Drunken with dusk, the other life forgotten,
    They haunt their tombs,
Mouldering, mouthing, mocking, mad and rotten,
    Around forgotten Coombes.

Coombes, less than two miles south of Steyning, boasts a tiny, eerie and gorgeous
Saxon church hidden off the road.

BOTOLPHS

The little marshlands of a shrunken river,
    Moist pasture-fields, a sense of sunken sun
    On a wet world of green, slight rills that run
Riverward, fieldward, loosely, and the quiver
Of tiny sea-winds: Botolphs. The sweet shiver
    Of virgin Spring is marvelously won
    Here in the lush; zones soon to be undone,
The promise of what Summer will deliver.

Bright grey and tender green; a silver light
    Set in a stream; a little dewy world,
Too young for gold, for summer-love too slight;
    A little maiden-ecstasy close-curled;
A wet sweet land of dream in a blue night
    Of lightest sleep; a murmuring emerald.

*Just up the Adur from Coombes, Botolphs is an 11th-century church a mile
from Steyning.*

THE BARROW

O ver long-mouldered flesh and bone and marrow,
    Beneath the yellows of the sunset-clouds,
There lies a grave, long, mystic, green and narrow,
    That some forgotten savage form enshrouds;
Right on the hill-top, far from home and harrow:
The evening winds play softly round the barrow.

Sunset and silence and the eternal wonder
    Of life up here three thousand years ago;
They are not far, those days, not far asunder
    From now: the same delicious breezes blow;
The fieldfares' fathers loved the hill; and under
Grows the same grass, sprung from the earth's primal thunder.

Man's eyes turn to the sunset, wistly skimming
    The evening sky; and everything remains;
Round the old hill are twittering fieldfares rimming;
    The night-wind cries: the dead bones and their banes,
The old stones and their stains, stay; never dimming
The earth's fire-heart: the fount of life stays brimming.

Turn downwards to the village in the valley;
    Sit with your feet before the fendered fire,
Sipping the Sussex brew: and musically
    The crickets sing; the kettle, evening's lyre.
Accompanies; the curtains draw, and sally
Forth to the mind-home where the old lives rally.

And there outside it's night; the hill is starred,
    Just as it was three thousand years ago:
Take down your Homer, with a gold regard
    To old Odysseus. Say; was it not so
When brave Maeonides, a blind, fierce bard,
Fared out to sing – blind, with a sight unmarred?

There lies the barrow, shining in the moonlight,
    It is out there, out on the homing hill;
Clasp close the treasured dream, the softly-strewn light
    That 'lumes your endless mind; oh! it is still
The same old Truth! The same old, wondrous rune-light
Shall lead you through its moonlight and its noon-light.

Outside the world flows on; tonight the falling
    Dews make the hill all sodden; through the elms
The same wind blows; far off the sea is calling:
    The same old dreams: the same old roystering realms
Of men and wars; the same old pains are galling;
Outside it's night; the world has hushed its brawling.

There lie the bones and sinews, nerve and marrow
    Mouldered past dust, dead in the living night;
There is the tomb, divorced from home and harrow:
    There the old Chieftain lies; a village light
Gleams, and a blind is drawn. There is the narrow
Old mystic grave. Homer! There lies the barrow!

IVORY

In ivory are Canterbury bells;
    The soaring bee's a golden argosy;
Yellow and gold; yellow and golden spells
    In ivory.

The yellow-luted cuckoo on a sea
    Of daffodils; the fluting of bee-cells;
Beatitudes in ivory melody.

This is the song that sways and swirls and swells
    Softly in summer-dawns; an ivory key
To the green Gate where dwell ineffables
    In ivory.

DECLINE

Now droops the soft year to her dusk Nadir;
    The sun wearies of wooing; life is stilled,
    Silent: old Contemplation is fulfilled;
Now is the Fall of Time, the Under-year.
The skies are tender ere they grow severe;
    The skies are tender, passion having willed
    Beyond endurance: all the air is chilled,
And mournful is the heavy atmosphere.

The year's inverted: even echoes dawn,
    But tenderly; love lies subdued and docile;
        Greenness is veiled; the grey-green earth is lush
With dew; on the sad lawn the laughing Faun
    Fleers at the unborn Spring; the earth's a fossil,
        And drooping low swings in the sunless hush.

EPILOGUE

From love to love,
 From hill to hill,
To rove and rove;
 This is my Will.

Until, until
 I shall return,
I thrill and thrill,
 I burn and burn.

For love I yearn
 While love I spill:
New love I learn
 By a Wind-mill.

Oh, wing you still,
 My wandering dove,
From hill to hill,
 From love to love.

SONGS
OF THE GROVES:

RECORD OF THE ANCIENT WORLD

Songs of the Groves: Records of the Ancient World
(Published anonymously.)
Victor B. Neuburg, author.
(Dennis West, wood-cut illustrations and cover design.)
The Vine Press, Steyning. 1921.

That Neuburg's prolific early-1920s period should wend its way towards the esoteric seems inevitable. The path from bawdy folksong to Romantic landscape and back to his formative love of all things classical and pagan was preordained. Just as *Swift Wings* is a tribute to the magic of place in Neuburg's life, *Songs of the Groves* is a rededication to the place of magic. Compare the cover art: Stanbrough's Sussex windmills, their 'swift wings' stilled in a breezeless image, on the side of a cut in the Downs; and on *Groves*, Dennis West's mash-up of classical, Biblical and occult symbology* into a framework of esoteric bait. West's art is meant to bring the viewer inside, through a portal, to some ancient knowledge, to the discovery of a new magick-with-a-'k'.

The Sussex landscape is still a key player in this book (just as pagan legends appeared in *Swift Wings*), but it is within a new framework, such as in 'Downwood', which celebrates Neuburg's beloved Chanctonbury Ring, the tree-ringed Iron Age hillfort high atop the South Downs just outside Steyning. But rather than homage to the still of its beeches, 'Downwood' is a chilling precursor to folk horror, imagining the 'little forgotten men' who 'worshipped ... forgotten things' with their 'blind forces / obsolete spells'. Such pagan pieces – be they of the Downs or the Druids; Diana or Dionysus – are the strength of *Songs of the Groves*. At times, Neuburg goes so far into his classicism as to make mediocre

---

* Prominent among the book's cover imagery is a swastika. In 1920s England, with influence from India commonplace, such an image would've still been seen everywhere from church walls to the Boy Scouts' Medal of Merit. Its use would not stop until the early-1930s as the German Nazi party's annexation of the image became more widespread.

translations of well-known Greek works, the act of translating becoming a mystical action itself.

Likewise, love is still on Vickybird's mind in *Songs of the Groves*, but this time it is often Love as positioned in relation to Will (in a potentially Crowleyite manner), or the rampant, Pan-like Spring-fever love that Neuburg adores from his classical and folk sources.

That's not to say that things weren't going well for the poet in affairs of the heart. He and Kathleen were splitting time between Sussex and London, where he had helped Kathleen obtain employment as dancer and choreographer Margaret Morris's secretary. In the summer of 1921, soon after *Songs of the Groves* was published, the couple spent time in Pourville, France, at Morris's famed summer school, where Loïs Hutton referred to him as 'Kathleen's young man' (this despite Neuburg being a decade older than Goddard and many of the other participants). There, in the evenings, Neuburg read poems from *Groves* to assembled luminaries-to-be including Morris and J.D. Fergusson, artists such as Hutton, Cedric Morris and Bertram Park, and the poet Edna St. Vincent Millay.

Neuburg's original introductions to the poems appear in italics at the top of the pieces.

EPIGRAPH

The olden Sun beyond the Hills
    Sinks, and the old Winds blow;
The same old splendid Passion thrills,
    The same new Splendours glow.
Look back! And may it be that you
Find Life and Love and Joy anew!

Once they were ours! They shall return:
The same old Fires anew shall burn!

DEDICATION

The breathless night is dark and blue,
    Sleeping without a stir or stain,
And underneath her dream peeps through
    Dawn, like a silver vein.

The water at our feet is still,
    The air is still; she reigns supreme,
A lyric rapture of the Will –
    Night, the eternal Dream.

There is no barque upon the stream,
    No single footfall goes or comes,
But all the world glides by, a dream
    Of dimly muffled drums.

So, curtained in her lucent blue,
    She sleeps without a stir or stain;
And underneath her dream peeps through
    Dawn, like a silver vein.

PROEM

An introduction to the Book: Being an Invocation to the Night Sky.

Fireflies glitter
Where glow-worms dwell,
Where thrushes twitter,
In the green dell:
In the blue night:
In the silver light.

　　The mantle of the Night is drawn
　　O'er lake and lawn for Earth's delight.

Dost thou not hear,
O delicate curved ear?
Sphere to sphere,
World to world,
Calls:
Waterfalls
Of light
Are uncurled.
Night
Dwells among the blue spaces,
In the wide places.
Hast thou not heard?
No solitary word
Came:
But all the spheres
Met in a single Flame
That flashed by
Our ears
Into the night sky.

There is
But one Globe:
She holds
All this
We call life
In her robe.
She unfolds
All bliss:
All strife:
All fate:
She is above
Hate
And love:
She is ours;
From her spring
All flowers
That bloom,
All birds
That sing,

All words,
All doom.
Her name
Is hidden in the Flame:
This is the word
I heard.
Wherefore I unfold
These songs of old.

     The mantle of the Night is drawn
     O'er lake and lawn for Earth's delight.

DOWNWOOD

*An Autumn Vesperal, the grey hues merging into Night and the distant sound
of the Sea.*

*The Hills become blurred, a light Rain falls, and before the final
Darkness there is a Vision of light low-browed men scudding amongst the gorse.
Mingled with the dream of forgotten Races, there is a motif of Reminiscence
and a Fireside.*

Now evening sways
    The boisterous sighing elms,
And the wind overwhelms
The barren hilly ways.
It is sobriety of earth,
The call
Of old dim ways to birth:
The fall
Of leaves; the nakedness of trees,
The breeze
Over the hills: an homily
Of the strong sea.
Swaying: swaying: swaying:
Dead leaves go and go,
Slow,
Slow blown by eddies of wind
Playing, playing,
Thinned, thinned,
Cold as a drift of snow
In an old barn at evening,
When fires are far,
And a single pale star
Shines, and a wing
Flutters in the hedge.
So darkness may bring
The world's edge,

Blue fading to grey,
With a solitary raven
Over bare fields:
Away and away
To the haven
That yields
Warm love, warm
From the dull evening storm.
There are pools on the hills,
Fearsome in evening light:
A breeze thrills and thrills
Them at night.
The distance is white
And grey.
It is a long way
Over to the sea.
Gulls fly over
From some pebbly cover
Sighingly; suddenly.
And suddenly wheatears arise
From a chalky place:
Like a shot before the eyes,
Like a flash before the face.
Who comes here must love lone
Places:
Where long-forgotten bone
Lies in the old spaces.
Death itself lives here.
The delicate panic fear
Is all around.
No sound
But is strange, out of time.
The ear
Never reaches to the rime;
The eye
Sees the idea die.

It is evening,
Night:
The tune
The winds sing
Is an old rune
Of an old rite.
Here,
In some long-dead year,
They worshipped, little forgotten men,
Forgotten things.
Then
Forgotten wings
Fluttered.
They live today
In memory,
Rising grey,
Unuttered,
From the eternal sea
Of man's mind,
Where everything dwells
That lived: blind
Forces,
Obsolete spells,
Like mountainous horses
Bearing
Vast iron bells.
Flaring, flaring
The old lights are dim:
Staring
Over the great grey rim,
I go
To my desire
By the warm fire.
But I know
The dream was true.
And stars come through:

But still,
My cheek upon my hand,
Looking into the hearth-flame,
I stand
On the old hill,
Chill,
In a forgotten land
With an unknown name.

DRUIDS

A Memory of an old Sacrifice. The sacred Victim is slain for an Omen. It is the End of an Age: being released the Ghost foretells the Passing of the old Worship, the Death of his Cult.
    The Sacrifice is made at the Summer Solstice, at Night.

In the soul's twilight broods the glittering core
Of wonder; all the stirring of the sea
At dawn, and all the yearning of the shore
At evening, and all the mystery
Of Time, at odds with his eternity.
Wherefore the shadows as they lift anew
From the waking mind disclose the ancient woods;
The white-robed Masters stare into the blue
Entrails of ravens: as dim multitudes
Of strange souls gather round, to watch the moods
Of large and yellow-silver flames of fire,
And brown-grey smoke, and perfumes of sweet breath.
Even so lightly once I struck the lyre
At evening, before a magic death.
Back from my breast I drew the heavy robe,
Baring the curving belly, the sun's globe.
The silver knife was over me: I lay

In ecstacy of life-in-death: away
Faded the silly world: again I knew
The source of living, as they shaved the hair,
From breast and belly and all; luminous blue
Swathed round me; I was dead, no longer there
Before the knife had split my navel: far
Away I heard arise the ancient prayer,
Scarcely I knew a pang. From some dim star
I saw: and how they caught the scarlet flood
That pulsed from gasping thighs: I saw the blood
Crimson the flame. Then suddenly there fell
The old gods glory on me. Earth was mud,
And I was swimming, easy as the spell
The priestly voices roared. Then, a white flash,
I stood before the flame, like living ash
Gifted with speech. The song died down, and I
Was the sole voice of that tremendous sky
Over the sacred wood. Now I knew all
The Druid mystery: the festival
Of blood was bared. It was my blood that gave
The answer of the night, the bitter call
Of death, responding of the restless wave
To life. Around me stared a living wall
Of waiting, hungry shadows, by that flame
Tempted to the old life. I was a lord
Of shadows, and a god. Then the Voice roared:
Speak! And I saw my body's last blood-spasm
As the old priests bent over it. A name
They skirled. Should I reply? I saw a chasm
Before the Altar, invisible to all
Of flesh. Then flared the thought: The altar's dead.
Then came the word: Woe! was the word I said;
It was an age's end. I saw them fall,
Fearful beneath a towering grey of sky;
This was the omen: Woe. An age to die,
I the last victim. So I passed from them

For ever, and I haunted the dark hem
Of the forest, for an age ere birth to rove,
The sacred Victim of an Holy Grove.
Then was I born anew; from that old birth
I culled this vision of forgotten earth.

PHILOMEL

*The Mythos of the Nightingale singing in dark woods by a Fountain: the song
tells of the Legend of Daulis, and of Pandion of Athens. Of the Moon-spell and
of Love Forgotten. And of the Ultimate Triumph of Love.*

*The Water gleams and bubbles in the Moonlight: the trilling Nightingale
sings on of her Passion: it is the Hour before Dawn on a Summer's Night.*

The spell of Philomel:
The moon through dark groves:
Wandering loves:
Such is the Spell.

Over the fallows
The sun has sunken deep:
The full moon has shone
Alone:
Now no star hallows
With silver light
The sleep
Of Night.

It was delight
Of swaying trees –
Elms, pines, cypresses;

A huge fountain, pale
In sombre moonlight, gleamed
Always. Philomel's tale
Was dreamed.
Moonrays slid sparkling,
Darkling,
Into the live water.

Pandion's daughter
Roves: roves: roves
The sacred groves.
Her blood is pale
As the tale
Of a virgin dying,
Lying
In yellow roses
And dark violets.

The wind never closes
Her song.
Never, never she forgets,
She who wanders
Long:
Buried in her regrets
She ponders
This mystery of Night
Without a star.

Far,
Far away
On the edge
Of the earth,
On a ledge
Overlooking the resounding sea,
Beyond night and day,
Above moon and sun,

Her thoughts run
Back, always back
To the black
Unutterable doom
She knew, she knew once:
From the old Tomb
Her orisons
Return,
To burn,
To burn her once again.
All her men
Pass before her,
Save him she seeks:
They adore her,
Yet she never speaks;
She waits, waits.
Shall the dark Fates
Restore her?
He is not there:
He is dead.
Where?

Overhead
Is no star
To guide her.
Beside her
Is the still
Water, chill,
Far, far
Sunken in the light
Of the great solitary Moon.

This is the night
Whereunder Philomel
Weeps.
This is the spell,

This is the noon
Whereunder Night sleeps.

Philomel
In the dark groves:
The spell
Of the lost loves
Trilling, trilling, trilling
Shrill and shrill
Throughout the willing
Softness of Night.

O dark hill
Of delight, delight!
O white,
Still
Splendour
Of the moon!
Tender, tender
In the rune
On her pale shield.
It is night:
The dark field
Grows bright.
O delight, delight!
Ye shall never yield!
It is night: night
And love's delight
Are over
The dark field,
In the clover,
Amidst the grass.
Pass! Pass
Into the pale moon
Never.
Stay strewn

Forever
Beneath the dark hills
In the pale fields:
It thrills and thrills,
The song:
Long and long,
Nor ever yields.

Ah! It is Love's delight:
The spell
Of Philomel
At night.

PANTHEA

A Tribute to Universal Nature, the Mother of all things, and the Source of all Life.
A Song of Woman and her Gifts: the Form Side of Earth, wherethrough Life enters and re-enters.
Of the Renewal of all Nature in the divine Motherhood of all Worlds. A Song of the Great Sea.

L eave thou the Islands of thy rearing: come
Unto the shadowy pools; Night's silver ring
Chains thee. Art thou not charmed? does evening
Not make thee silent? Yea: for thou art dumb
Here in thy Forest. Here are silences
Profounder than deep death. Thou canst not hear
Even the murmur of the Atmosphere
Borne on the wings of the delightful breeze
Of Night. The vermeil shadows change for thee,
For thee all form takes wing; the hour is fled;
There is no breath of life: all life is dead

Because of thee, and thy fair symmetry.
Have I not passed upon thy way? Have I
Not been within thee, and spent out my soul
In thee? Immortal, art thou not the whole
Of life, for whose sole lack all life would die?
Thou art the Way to life; from thee shall spring
What is to come; and in thy depths are laid
The Virgin's death: the passing of the Maid,
The fur, the down, the wings; yea! Everything
Is thine. And I, because indeed I love thee,
Because in joy I make myself thy slave,
Yearn utterly for thy warm, sheltering cave:
And entering find thy strange, dark moss above thee,
The scented down of love. Thy scent is sweeter
Than virgin honey from an earthly maid;
Soon shall I enter in thine evening shade,
And my rime fade into the unerring metre
Of thine eternal Song. Art thou not deep
As time? Is not thy touch more ripely rare
Than even the frondage of thy maidenhair?
Dost thou not bring at last the sweetest sleep
Wherefrom man wakes? Therefore I worship thee
In thine own woods: therefore I celebrate
Thee, who art lady of Love, and friend of Fate,
Who bringest all my fiercest joy to me.
What rhymth is like thine? Earth's pulses beat
In thee: the heart of love thou art. Thy touch
Brings life to softest birth: ah, grip! ah, clutch
Thy lover in thy force: lend him thine heat,
That, in thy soft entrancements lying dead,
He may arise anew, seek thee again:
Whence shall come glorious maids and laughing men,
To clasp and kiss. Is not thy hue more red
Than dawn's? Doth not thy tongue bring forth more joy
Than any song of man's? Dost thou not buoy
Men's souls with beauty? Are thy lips not fed

With man's fierce love? Maiden of Fate and Time,
I worship in truth and spirit: come to me
Who adore thee: I would give my soul to thee
For one swift echo of thee, one true rime
Of love. Come then! In thine enchanting cave
Thy lover spends his life for thee, my sweet
Immortal one! Thy lover at thy feet
Is lying now; nor vainly shall he crave
Thy wine, thy scent, thy touch. No more! For soon
Deep night must come, and I from hence shall pass
Over thy dewy woods, thy murmuring grass,
To lie at ease in thine enchanted swoon,
O lady of the Mirage and the Moon.

NIGHT-SONG OF BACCHUS

*Bacchus, accompanied by Pan and Silenus, passes through the woods upon an
Autumn Night. He sings his Dithyrambic Song of Wine and Love.*
　　*He tells of his Mission and of the Impending Ecstacy of the Earth. The
song ends with the Noon of Night.*

L eopards' eyes glow
　　In the underbrush of woods
As night falls slow
　　Upon her multitudes.

All her songs are mine,
　　All her stars are ours:
Mine is her wine,
　　Ours are her flowers.

Ring me a wreath,
  O Bacchantes mine,
While the tigers' teeth
  Are closing on the vine.

Who shall asperse us
  Among all mankind?
Know they my thyrsus
  When I be inclined?

I am god-drunken
  – Autumn mast and must –
When the sun is sunken
  The earth is driven dust.

Roll me a stave,
  Silenus and Pan!
Man is my slave;
  I am a Man.

Tigers ho! my tympans!
  Sway, my cymbals ho!
All mine is man's,
  Man's all below.

The red flame of vision
  From the lees of wine
Is mine, is Elysian,
  Is mine! is mine !

Pentheus, rude
  At my Mysteries,
Was torn and chewed,
  Wine, O my lees !

The Autumn sun is sunken
  Behind the ivy leaves:
I, wet and drunken,
  Come with the sheaves.

Harvest disdaining,
  Mine is the wine !
Lees drown-draining:
  The wine is mine !

Pan, come between us !
  Silenus, here !
Hither, Silenus !
  Pan, dost hear?

Lean o' my shoulder,
  Darling of the must !
Never grow older !
  Take me on trust !

Come, see my cars run
  Greased by the vine !
I make the stars run
  Dripping with wine !

Free men for Liber !
  Dionysus Ho !
From Thamesis to Tiber,
  From Padua to Po !

I was of Khem,
  And I was a Greek,
And I love them
  That bouse without a leak.

Swill it! transmute it !
  Hearken to my drums !
Never dispute it:
  Take it as it comes !

Hymen I father !
  When ye swim in wine,
My spirit is to gather;
  I am thine, and thine !

Ah, Night my sweetest !
  Stay yet with me !
When ye are fleetest
  Ye hold most ecstacy !

So, sweet my slaves !
  Masters of the must !
Sing me my staves !
  See my horns upthrust !

Sing so the Moon !
  I am the Sun !
Day comes too soon,
  Too soon night is done.

All the stars are mine !
  Bacchantes, hear !
Mine is your wine,
  With the kiss behind the ear !

Ho! for Bacchanalia
  Whereat to boast and bouse,
In the penetralia
  Of my forest house !

Come, O my starry
    Ones of wood and spring !
Come, ye here may marry,
    Love and swill and sing !

Borne by my beasts,
    Tamed to my cars,
I lighted all the East's
    Ecstacy of stars.

They called me never;
    But Dionysus came,
Whence earth forever
    Is lighted by my flame.

I was the new god
    Of wine and ecstacy;
Now I am the true god
    Of the Great Sea

Ho! It is ended !
    Night is fully come:
With night I am blended;
    With night I am dumb.

So down through the woods
    Dionysus came;
All their multitudes
    Bowed at his name.

Night fell slowly;
    The song arose: and far
Fell his light, the holy
    Murmur of a Star.

A SONG OF STARS

Of the Secret of Life and its Incommunicability. The Unknown Word of the
Stars that would be the Key to Life.
Life lives as Stars die; and is hence Immortal.

The little moons of evening
    Are framed in pine, are sapphire-set;
The little winds awake and sing
    Slow songs of violet.
Green earth contracts while pale moons grow,
    Softly and slow.

Each moon for our delight has heard
    Songs of swift stars, awake to love:
Violet veil and flowered word,
    Patterned in deeps above,
Veil and reveal those blossoms set
    In violet.

Unveil the mystery of grass,
    The wonder of dark woods, the call
Of noisy eagles as they pass –
    O aery waterfall !
O little moons that are so young,
    Is it not sung?

Who knows? The breeze reveals the dawn;
    The little moons unveil the sea;
Wild clover-scent makes emerald lawn
    No less a mystery.
Whoso hath heard hath truly heard
    The secret Word.

No word reveals it, and no eye
    Beholds it, and no ear may know:
Yet in some sense the sensient sky
    Is conscious of a glow
Beneath, beneath in wheeling earth,
    Nor death, nor birth.

For life is set 'twixt birth and death,
    And Love lies throned 'twixt death and birth,
This is the word the dark sky saith
    Unto revolving earth;
The incommunicable word,
    Unsaid, but heard.

Winds sing, but in a key unknown,
    And rolling rivers rush to tell
Nothing: the singing in the stone
    Is still no miracle;
The touch of fur and the bee's wing
    Tell no new thing.

Yet in the deeps calls star to star,
    The grass sings loudly to the sky,
And planets know not any bar;
    Each unto each they cry.
Shall Art reveal the word? Who knows
    How the song grows?

Strange eyes peer out from rainy leaves,
    To tulip-tongues strange lips reply,
And phantom planets roll where heaves
    A strange white aether-sky:
Tenuous themes are theirs, who skim
    That secret rim.

Every lip to every ear?
    Never, while the little moons
Slide along their easy sphere;
    And singing summer noons
Holds no hint of things. Who knows
    How a star grows?

In every star a burning core
    Glows: the star cools, and life is born
Anew: Love comes; with him once more
    Come man and rain and corn:
Life grows in heat; but stars grow cold
    As Love grows bold.

And at the end? As the stars pale,
    In strange new forms life still will glow;
This is the secret song; the tale
    Whereby lives swell and grow.
As the stars cool life in new form
    Shall still be warm.

THE GARDEN OF PYTHAGORAS
BY WAY OF APOLOGUE

The Gateway of Remembrance lies
Deeplier hid than thought or sense,
Where the Third Eye behind the eyes
Directs the eyes' intelligence.
There the Eye knows how chance and change,
Success and failure, turn and pass,
Meeting and greeting oft: to range
The Garden of Pythagoras.

As the little winds blow through the ivy, so blows the wind of memory through the lives upon the wall of life: children of the Sun, every breeze is a messenger, an angelos. Were it not so we should cease to be, for being is becoming: and the End of becoming is unknown to man.

Understanding is a gift of the Sun; memory a gift of the wind. Æons ago we we were motes of dust dancing in a primeval storm; now we are stars moving in a heaven of thought and dream: impinging; refracting; responding: dust still; but dust Informed.

The Garden I found was enclosed by an old wall, and veined by seven rivers: it was understanding of separation to be there. Time failed me, and time again was born. I was there for no time; yet was everything plain to me in my sojourning. When I left I forgot; remembering only at intervals, at odd times, I know not why.

Now the wind shifted to the east; and from the Sun-gates a golden eagle flew through the Inane: he was the messenger of Jove. This was his message:

A King lay sleeping in his garden; kisses were upon his lips, wine was in his heart, upon his brow was understanding. It was Summer, and in his dreams he heard the singing of bees, the growing of grass. And it seemed to him that the Reason of life was plain to him; he was in a gold sphere, spinning, spinning: and each thread was a kind of life, and each strand was a part of an whole tapestry. He weaved at random; at length he weaved the great gold eagle before him, and I was that eagle, and I was there in the garden, and I was that King.

And I remembered, for I was in the Garden: when I passed through the Gate I passed as King and as an eagle, the messenger of a King: so I explained it to my Self. But my Self was silent, for He knew all; and all memory was to him as a mockery: for was He not beyond time, having been in the garden?

An old poet told me of his craft. He said: I too have seen the eagle; I too have become him; but I knew only when I was far hence: but you know now. What else is there indeed? I was silent. He went on: That was the true Pythagoras, who carried his garden with him: for he was himself a garden; enclosed; contained; nourished by the Sun.

Greece, he said, was known to him once; but Pythagoras told him to forget it. For only so, he said, can Greece be reborn; for we seek not what we remember; only what we forget. Hence man quaffs before birth the waters of Lethe, of forgetfulness. But we who remember, are we not poets and artists and dreamers? The world hates us; but then how rare is understanding! Kings can not come at it; and if they could they would lose all joy in life.

The old poet left me, and I pondered upon his identification with life. I had once a friend who had written forty books of wisdom, and knew no more of love than an amœba. So I turned to write of simple things; but like a lamp in a shrine my initiation shone through, and I had to write, whether I would or no, of the illumination that is the motive of all sensient life.

A bramble-bush became the World-Tree; a herd of cows one of the hairs upon the head of the Great Bull of the Universe. I could not escape, therefore, the spell of Eden and of Horus. All had become divine; and men charged me with obscurity when all life lay before me as an open book, to be read at my own will. They talked of sheep whilst I was communing with Horus: they chaffered timber when I was kissing the Great Mother. They hated me for hating their stupid rivalries and their low vision: but as for me, I loved them, for that eventually they would attain to understanding.

So I retired beneath the olive-trees in the garden of Pythagoras, and the eagle dropped a wreath of myrtle upon me: and again I was the King; for my maidens brought me their kisses, and my friends their wine; and so I sang to them and loved them all.

And I was crowned King until the End of the Æon.

COLOPHON

The Poet seeks refuge in his Garden from the Disorders of his Time: meditating, he foretells a Return to Natural Things, and the Spring of the Spirit: and to a renewed worship of Youth and Love.

The Poem, as the Book, ends in the complete Assurance of a New Age, and of a Rebirth of Beauty.

The tall flowers
Of the hollyhocks
Are not yet won:
But we get
Wall-flowers,
And the silver locks
Of mignonette
Will come anon.

April grows May,
With a pale
Blue pavilion,
And a tale
Of vermillion
Polyanthus,
Or thus
They say.

The modern time
Is full of riot
And incoherent regret:
So one retires
For one's rime
To the quiet
Of a cigarette,
Cool amid the spring fires.

It is delicious,
Or so it seems
To me,
To leave the strange
Dreams
Of psychology
And of psycho-analysis
For the kiss
Of a quiet April sun:
And to range
Far away
From the vicious
Schemes
Of our day.

Soon
There will be won
A quiet moon
Above the pale green
Of the garden.
The soft hours
Harden
Their flowers
In the serene
Majesty
Of the clear
Year.

We
Shall return
 – Or so it seems to me –
To learn
The original mystery
Of the birth
Of the year:
Of the earth,

That strange sphere
Of striped green:
Clear –
Speckled –
Lean –
Deckled
At the edges
 – Like some books –
With ragged hedges.

And mysterious looks
Come out of the night:
And bright,
Strange
Sounds
Range
The grounds.
Strange eyes, too, peer

From the Spring
Of the year;
Strange voices sing
As well;
One can hear
As in a spell.
But no-one sees,
Except a few,
Like, maybe,
You
And me,
The new
Mysteries,
That are,
I suppose
 – O Silver Star ! –
The things

That youth brings:
The song of the rose

Unborn, unsprung
That is sung
At the close
Of day
— The Yogin hour —
When the last ray
Of the sun
Closes like a flower,
And all life seems done.

Let the pen run
Yet a little
Still
As it will:
Thought is so brittle;
Soon
It will break
Beneath

The starry wreath
Of the moon,
Whose hidden fire
(For the Poet's sake)
— For it is nearing noon —
May inspire
The words
I spill
In little rushes
From my quill,
As young thrushes,
Just-fledged birds,
Are shaken
From an elm

Thus doth thought awaken
To overwhelm
The mind.

But I
Find
At the moment
The pale sky
Kind:
So – without comment –
Here I close,
As suddenly as a rose
When the warm
Air portends
A storm.
So
The song ends,
And I go.

SONGS
OF A
SUSSEX TRAMP

Songs of a Sussex Tramp
Rupert Croft-Cooke, author.
The Vine Press, Steyning. 1922.

Author Rupert Croft-Cooke (1903-1979) would be considered relatively prolific if he'd written nothing but his autobiography, which, remarkably, spans more than 20 volumes. But that was far from the end of it: under his own name Croft-Cooke produced a corpus that would make most writers sick with envy, including scores of novels, plays, poetry and a slew of nonfiction from lit-crit to cookery. And, under his pseudonym Leo Bruce, the author produced what might as well be a second body of work consisting of a few dozen detective novels and short-story collections.

Yet Croft-Cooke's life in letters began humbly: with *Songs of a Sussex Tramp*, published by The Vine Press and printed by Victor Neuburg in Steyning. The book is notable not only as its author's first book accepted for publication, but as the first Vine Press book to begin life outside of the Cottage. A 17-year-old Rupert Croft-Cooke had gotten wind of these odd printings coming out of Steyning, and in particular its *Swift Wings*-esque interest in Sussex poetry. 'I wanted with consuming impatience to "be a writer"', Croft-Cooke later stated, and he decided on a course of action. After all, hadn't he walked the county well, like Belloc before him? Lived, if only for a few days, the tramp's life of W.H. Davies? And, surely, couldn't he refit some of his boyhood poems of impatient love and wanderlust to include Sussex place names?

The poems Croft-Cooke bundled off to Vine Press – its proprietor unmet; its purpose unsought – became, almost immediately, *Songs of a Sussex Tramp*:

'[Neuburg] seemed to take it for granted that he was to publish the poems and without saying so spoke of a de luxe edition signed, remarked that I had read too much Swinburne, asked if I thought the book should be illustrated. There was nothing about terms; there was nothing factual at all.'

Neuburg believed in the young poet, printing more than 600 copies of *Songs of a Sussex Tramp*, and garnering relatively decent publicity through newspapers in Sussex and Kent. And while one may argue that the 'Sussex' and 'Tramp' aspects of the book began as something of a falsehood, some of the 'Songs' therein do rise to the occasion and join the respectable Belloc-ian tradition of writers traipsing the South Downs. Croft-Cooke's most important contribution to The Vine Press story, however, is probably through his chapters on the Vickybird in *The Glittering Pastures*, one of his autobiographies, in which he contrasts – and, depending on which you believe, dispels – some of Arthur Calder-Marshall's better-known depictions of life at Vine Cottage.

The Neuburgs that Croft-Cooke saw were more equal and less poverty-stricken; they were more contented with their lot. He found Victor to be optimistic and joyful in his eccentricities – not cowed into hiding by his past, although perhaps occasionally longing for its reveries. What's more, as he says in *Glittering Pastures*, he instantly *liked* Vickybird, who treated the teenager as a poet, an individual and an equal.

An unnamed issue got between Croft-Cooke and Vine Press for a few years, though they rekindled their friendship before Neuburg left Steyning, and the book was rarely mentioned after. But as part of a small but well-honed set of books of poems of the Sussex landscape, *Songs of a Sussex Tramp* remains key to the early Vine Press output.

PREFACE

I am a tramp.
 It is no disgraceful thing nowadays to be a tramp,
especially if you can lay claim to being a literary one.
I often wonder whether, in my wanderings in Sussex, I shall
meet one of my own kind, for so many seem to choose this
county. Why not? For in Sussex there are still good-nature and
hospitality, kindly firesides and country beer, simple men and
natural women.

 These little songs are all that I can give you of the good
things that I have gained by hard walking and love. For though
I have gained so much, the things are intangible and almost
incommunicable.

 I cannot write a deeper or a higher hope than that in my
songs may be found the spirit of Sussex.

OLD HASTINGS

SONNET

Alone I climb the hill and see the town
 Sombre and leaden; here and there a spire
 Or a small turret juts acuter, higher –
A road that puckers through it like a frown;
A single cart that rattles up and down;
 A wisp of chimney-smoke, some struggling fire;
 And faint the shouting of an early crier –
All colours moulded in a misty brown.

I love it, this old town, wedged with such grace
    Between its hills. On one the castle seems
        To hold suggestions of eternity;
This corner of the world – a simple face
    Lovely in smiling age – a haunt of dreams –
        A bit of England as she used to be!

THE DOWNS

Oh, loud is the call of the woodland to me –
Appealing the call of the moorland!
And mighty the mystical call of the sea
From Selsey away to the Foreland.
Sweet are the ways of the ocean,
Fair are the ways of the towns,
But falls on the ear, delightful to hear,
The magical call of the Downs.
        Away to the Downs!
        Away to the Downs!
    Love, life and laughter –
        Away to the Downs!

Men say there's a heaven unmatched by the earth
Where we may be happy hereafter,
And the place as they see it has little for mirth,
And little or nothing for laughter.
    Where the oceans are all made of jasper,
    And the commonest people wear crowns,
    If they'd been there to see, the world would agree
    'Twere better to stay on the downs!
        Away on the Downs!
        Away on the Downs!
    Love, life and laughter
        Away on the Downs!
Seaford.

BIRLING GAP

Along towards the light-house under the cliffs I came to a halt on a
wild, tossing morning.

I tread a mile or so along the shore
And watch the long waves rolling to their doom,
While over me the cliffs, appalling, loom;
The seagulls shriek in swooping choruses,
And sweeping by, the great sea tempests roar;
The waves dash higher, cool my face with spray,
The scene gives now what time will take away –
The heroism of Greek Manliness!
The love for battle and the muscling strokes
Of windy battlings; now, I feel the ire
Of all the elements that pass me by;
The threatening cliffs, the tempest and the sea,
I face them with their own begotten fire.
It is one aspect of God's mighty plan
To give the elements power to make a man:
I feel a man! wild for heroic deeds –
I feel outside the world's desires and creeds!
This lone tempestuous shore has given me
A longing for immensity and strength;
I stand, like Neptune, on the rocks, and see
Over a vastly spread, unlived-on length.
Oh! for the waves of strength, the winds of bliss,
Oh! for the spirit of true manliness!

WAVES

I had got into a town; a rare happening, but when rain is perpetual
there is always a call to civilisation, and Brighton is, of course,
distinctly civilised.
        One afternoon the sun came out suddenly over the sea.

Wild sea in winter sunlight –
    A halo of thin spraying
Around the fallen heads
    Of king-like waves.

No boat to break the endless
Uninterrupted vision
Of laughter-shouting waves
    Of English seas.

When God divided waters
It was by winter sunlight
With waves that longed to reach him
    Uplifting high.

LEWES GAOL

Stand here on the downs, the downs that are free –
Fragrant and free they slope upward and fall;
Can you imagine what you would see
        Over the wall?

The wind here has traversed the county – you hear it –
Gathered its fragrance and carried it all
Hither to greet you, unable to bear it
        Over the wall.

Here the birds sweep and the landscape is blotless;
Sea-gulls come hither, veer upward and call;
Does the sound carry? Is the sky spotless
      Over the wall?

Over the wall, do they think in this fashion,
Dream of this view as the days onward crawl,
Till dead are ambition and mem'ry and passion
      Over the wall?

Do they wake in the morning and smell the sweet clover,
Look up and wonder and madden and fall?
O Wind! O breather of Life! Reach over,
      Over the wall!

Mortals who call themselves free in their prison,
Their prison of earth, so wide and so small,
Are they not manacled till they have risen
      Over the wall?

LARKSPUR:

A LYRIC GARLAND

Larkspur: A Lyric Garland
Victor B. Neuburg, Editor-Author.
(Anthology attributed to real and assumed names.)
Dennis West, woodcut illustrations.
The Vine Press, Steyning. 1922.

Lillygay had been relatively well received, with good notices in general and with no less than GK Chesterton's *The New Witness* citing it as containing "the stock of an undying spirit". Another anthology of writing from the public domain seemed an obvious move. But this time, there would be a catch: more than a third of the 'authors' would be Neuburg writing under pseudonyms in the anachronistic styles represented within the book.

Like in his other edited volumes, Larkspur represents an eccentric taste in what Neuburg might have considered 'sempiternal' English-language verse: moments of pastoral bliss and Romantic love sit side-by-side with thinly veiled tales of debauchery in one of Vine Press's volleys in the war against a dominant prudish conservatism. John Keats and Aphra Behn share space with folksongs from *The English Dancing Master* and other traditional ballads; the editor even foreshadows a future Vine Press title by referencing de Musset. In his prologue, Neuburg sets these pieces out as immortal; as the influence upon 'mood and mode', rather than being subject to it. That he would include several of his own tales and retellings within such a set might've been an accidental hat-tip to modernism, with its prankster impulse and love of pseudonym and heteronym. Or it could be Neuburg's belief that – as he sets out from the beginning – such works are, in fact, reflecting a god-light as the moon might do, rather than being unique and self-created masterpieces.

In 1922, with first his aunt and now his roommate, Hayter Preston, having vacated their use of the home, Vickybird and his new bride were truly ensconced in Vine Cottage. Kathleen gave up her Margaret Morris job, and London with it, and the pair lived largely off Neuburg's small allowance. Vine Press even generated some level of income, through sales and, more importantly, printing jobs for businesses and individuals in the region. It was a happy time, apparent from *Larkspur*'s dedication with its repetitive references to 'roses' (as in both the 'Sempiternal Rose', and Kathleen Rose Neuburg née Goddard).

Neuburg's contributions to *Larkspur* are referenced in Jean Overton Fuller's biography, and are fairly obvious once known: besides the familiar, top-and-tail unattributed pieces, Chrystopher Crayne, Paul Pentreath, Harold Stevens, Lawrence Edwardes, Arthur French and Nicholas Pyne were all written or rewritten by Neuburg. The pieces by 'Crayne', 'Pyne' and 'Edwardes' play at Vickybird's beloved anachronisms – extraneous e's and y's and hey-nonny-nonny's all 'round – while 'French' and 'Pentreath' sing of the 19th century. 'Harold Stevens' could almost be a stab at something more contemporary and more Neuburgian; it wouldn't have been out of place in *Songs of the Groves*.

Like *Lillygay*, *Larkspur*'s influence fell most strongly on the ear of two songwriters. Peter Warlock would be inspired to use 'The Milk-Maids' for his song 'Milkmaids'. (At a 1929 performance of Warlock's song in Steyning, this centuries-old lyric is noted as being "by a local author … Mr Victor Neuburg.") Another member of Vickybird's circles, the composer Roger Quilter, used a genuinely original text for his song 'Trollie Lollie Laughter'; rather than 'Nicholas Pyne' the song is attributed to Victor B. Neuburg. (In a tip to Bacchus that Victor would've loved, baritone Mark Stone, speaking of his 2020 recording of the song, says appreciatively that he couldn't make it work until realising that Quilter had written it after he'd 'spent a bit too long in the Savoy cocktail bar…')

DEDICATION

TO THE ROSE IMMORTAL

When ducks gabble home through the meadows,
 Ere blue noons fade to grey,
Ere the moon leads out her shadows,
  The last song slips away.

Philosophy fades in the phases
 Of the changeless-changing moon;
Death cowers under the daisies,
  While over the fields laughs noon.

The year-times fail and falter
 Through the world's strange garden-close;
Faiths fall and die by the altar
  Of the Sempiternal Rose.

So to the Rose of Beauty,
 The Heart in each Star impearled,
Is sung the Artist's duty,
  The Poet's love for his world.

PROLOGUE

There are fashions in the arts, but Art knows no fashion. The moon is older than Sappho, younger than de Musset. The mood passes, the mode passes, but that which informs mood and mode remains, by the wit of the gods.

The flashes of god-light in this little book would have been as intelligible to Adami and to Menes as they are to us; their meaning will remain undisturbed for many æons. The shadows change their shapes and fly; the Light is one and immortal. It is the word of the gods to man.

THE MILK-MAIDS

Walkeing betimes close by a green wood side,
      Hy tranonny, nonny with hy tranonny no;
A payre of lovely milk maides there by chance I spide,
      With hy tranonny nonny no, with tranonny no.

One of them was faire, as fair as fair might bee;
      Hy tranonny, nonny with hy tranonny no;
The other she was browne, with wanton rowling eye,
      With hy tranonny no, with tranonny no.

Syder to make sillibubs they carryed in their pailes;
      Hy tranonny, nonny with high tranonny no;
And suggar in their purses hung dangling at their tailes,
      With hy tranonny nonny no, with tranonny no.

Wast-coats of flannell and pettycoats of redd,
      Hy tranonny, nonny with high tranonny no;
Before them milk white aporns, and straw-hats on their heads,
      With hy tranonny nonny no, with tranonny no.

Silke poynts, with silver taggs, about their wrists were shown.
    Hy tranonny, nonny with high tranonny no;
And jett-Rings with poesies – "Yours more than his owne,"
    With hy tranonny nonny no, with tranonny no.

And to requite their lovers' poynts and rings,
    Hy tranonny, nonny with high tranonny no;
They gave their lovers bracelets, and many pretty things,
    With hy tranonny nonny no, with tranonny no.

And there they did get gownes all on the grasse so green,
    Hy tranonny, nonny with high tranonny no;
But the taylor was not skilfull, for the stitches they were seen,
    With hy tranonny nonny no, with tranonny no.

Thus having spent the long summer's day,
    Hy tranonny, nonny with high tranonny no;
They took their nut browne milk pailes, and so they came away,
    With hy tranonny nonny no, with tranonny no.

Well fare you, merry milk maids that dable in the dew,
    Hy tranonny, nonny with hy tranonny no;
For you have kisses plenty, when Ladyes have but few,
    With hy tranonny nonny no, with tranonny no.

– Dr. James Smith

THE AMOROUS SHEPHERDESS

The birdes they sing on every tree,
    The throstle, cockow, larke;
The starling calls all daye to me,
    Nyghtgales throwe the darke:
        When my sweet Swaine
        Returnes againe
Togethere we will harke.

The greene bryghte Yeare againe is newe
    With Springe's swete Crystenyng;
The skyes are mottl'd whyte and blew,
    The leaves are listening
        For newe softe raine
        To come againe
And make then glystenynge.

O swete new Yeare! O come sweet fere!
    Whyte Shepherde of the Plaines!
O come my deare! Thy love is here,
    And waits the silver straines
        Of thy sweete Pipe;
        Nowe Sprynge is rype,
Come with the firste newe Raines.

– Chrystopher Crayne

THE BALLAD OF LYONESSE

They were living, laughing, loving,
     But they all got laved;
Some of them were roving,
     And they got saved.

Was it a mantis,
     Rebeck at his breast,
Singing of Atlantis
     Lost in the West?

When the skies darken
     Out on Western-meer,
Then, when you hearken,
     What do you hear?

Hear the bells tolling?
     There were lost six-score;
Hear the cries rolling
     In to the shore?

And they heard it nearing
     As they lay at ease
With their women, fleering
     At anger of the seas.

Surge-boom! Urge-boom!
     The hill-waves go
Crashing on to man's doom,
     Urging hugest woe.

Living, loving,
     What is man's distress?
Green Death is roving

Where once was Lyonesse.
Loving, living
With women and with ease,
There is no forgiving
Of anger of the seas.

Cockrows incessant,
Kine that low and stumble,
Wide-eyed, whitening peasant,
Hear ye the rumble?

Yea! See the herdsmen
Rivalling the cows;
Only god-drunk wordsmen
Look with easy brows.

Waiting, waiting;
What is it to fly?
See Venus rise in hating,
Hiding all the sky!

Men bore their treasures
In hot brown hands;
There lie their pleasures
With them in the sands.

Women bore their treasures
Tugging at the breast;
Now they take their leisures
Far in the West.

Some lay in child-birth;
There they lie to-day:
Oh, 'twas a wild birth
Of the sea-spray.

Venus for anger
    Of her lost rites
Rose from her languor
    In the lack of lights.

Nay! Men shall fear me,
    Witness of the foam;
They shall know me, they shall hear me,
    Ere the gods go home.

– Paul Pentreath

THE YELLOW MOON

A midst the dark penumbrous
    Slow green foliage,
Vast, vast and slumbrous,
    She dallies for an age. –

Our Moon of Vision Valley,
    Light of Yellow Blaze,
Sombrely to rally
    Men of forgotten days.

Surely once they hear her,
    Slowly as she sings?
Surely once they near her,
    Softly as she swings?

Down in her palace
    She lights them all again;
In sleep they taste her chalice,
    The strange sleeping men.

They savour love long over,
    Superannuate Grail,
As over evening clover
    Outpours the dreamy tale.

Longer may they slumber,
    Nor let them yet return –
Moon-children without number,
    Men who are born to burn.

Stay not to watch them sleeping,
    All-conscious that they sleep;
They wake not yet to weeping,
    Whatever creatures creep.

They lie there; let them linger
    Until they hear the Wings,
Nor twang with wanton finger
    The old exciting strings.

Moon of Vision Valley,
    They must be born again:
But let them drowse and dally
    Yet, the sleeping men.

Leave them to their slumber,
    For they must wake anew,
Your children without number,
    Who bear the curse of you.

– Harold Stevens

GYLES AND JILLE

L illies for Love!
    Roses for Will!
        Where do you hide?
        Where do you bide?
Stars slant above
    The windy old hill,
    Do you love me still?
    Listen: oh, shrill –
        Hey! Ho!

Roses ripe-red!
    Lillies pure-pale!
        Where do you grow?
        Where do you blow?
Stars overhead,
    Over the vale,
    Your light shall not fail
    Down in the dale –
        Hey! Ho!

Winding the way to you!
    – Shout when you're near!
        Oh, we shall meet again!
        Oh, we shall greet again!
What shall I say to you?
    – What I would hear!
    Clear and more clear
    The song to my ear –
        Hey! Ho!

Gyles, oh, the Lad for me!
    Oh, and my Jille!
        Still you'll be there?

Still will you dare?
Be you still glad for me?
Up on the hill!
Still shall we thrill –
Thrill and be still –
Hey! Ho!

– Laurence Edwardes

BOWPOTS

B ravely blow the bowpots at Rookscaw in June!
    Bravely blow the bowpots in Honeysuckle Hollow!
Bravely blow the bowpots: Summer's here, and soon
    The bale-fires' flare on the hills will follow.

Honey-bees are hunting: the leaded diamond panes
    Are scarlet with geraniums; it's Rookscaw June;
Rookscaw June, interpolate with rains;
    Spring thunder's over: Summer's hot and soon.

Diamond geraniums; flaming purple flags;
    Blue sky veiled with aftermath of rains;
Lilies lie low, and the boom-bee sags
    Homeward, heavy with his honey-first gains.

Bravely blow the bowpots, gravely green the ways lie
    On the sunny hill-sides at Rookscaw in June;
Bravely blow the bowpots, hot and hard the ways lie
    Over all the greenwood: Summer's come soon.

– Arthur French

TROLLIE LOLLIE

Trollie lollie laughter!
    Swallows skim the sky;
Nightingales come after
    When the moone's up high.

When the golden moone comes
    Over the trees
Soone soone soone comes
    Cupid ore the leas.

Over the west the lighte falls
    When the daye dyes;
Soone soone Night falls
    From the somer skyes.

Trollie lollie laughter!
    See the sonne falle!
Love comes after
    With the moone's madrigall.

Darke boughs are bending
    Lovers above;
See the lovers wendinge
    The woode waye for love.

Galatea, Phyllis,
    Lais, Phylador,
Iris, Amaryllis,
    Alexis, Amyntor.

They know the good waye
    Uppe throughe the trees;
The moone-darke woode way,
    Cupid in the breeze.

Trollie lollie laughter,
    Dian rules the skye,
Lovers follow after
    To clip and claspe and sighe.

Hearken, shephearde's darling,
    How the songes swell!
The Sunne charmed the starlinge,
    The Moone wooes Philomell.

Trollie lollie lollie,
    Swallows skim the skye;
Lovers fulle of folly
    Linger laughing bye.

– Nicholas Pyne

EPILOGUE

For the New Age

When planets clash together
    To form a Birth of fire,
To inform the flaming heather,
    To make green hills aspire –
The amorous soft turtle,
    The dolphin gleaming gold,
See worlds burst their kirtle,
    Waters burst their hold.

So wind-and-water weather,
     With the golden-manëd Sire,
String-up in sunny tether
     Earth's seven-stringëd lyre:
So shall new thunders hurtle,
     So love's new buds unfold,
So strange young planets spirtle
     As love springs from their mould.

Upper star and nether
     Meet in star desire;
Fur and fin and feather
     In mingling flame untire:
May all girt zones ungirtle,
     All blushing breasts grow bold!
Under Venus' myrtle
     Earth's joy be uncontrolled!

COLOPHON

L ittle winds whistle
     Along the way,
The strong brown thistle
     Makes holiday.

Little winds whisper
     Through the trees,
The sea-scent's crisper
     In the breeze.

Rose-leaves rustle
	And poppy-leaves fall;
Oak-boughs tussle
	And rude rooks brawl.

Starlight's coming!
	Evening thrills
At the sea-winds, drumming
	From the Hills.

For little winds whistle
	From the sea,
To bring the missel
	New harmony.

And little winds muffle
	Owl cries in the eaves,
And little winds ruffle
	The early sheaves.

Little wind! little wind! you
	Are mine; I adore you:
The sea is behind you,
	The dawn is before you.

NIGHT'S TRIUMPHS:

SONGS OF NATURE

Night's Triumphs: Songs of Nature
Ernest Osgood Hanbury (1852-1927), author.
The Vine Press, Steyning. 1924.

The publication of *Night's Triumphs*, a book of nature poetry by Ernest Osgood Hanbury, marks a potentially important moment in the life of The Vine Press. There's no question that Hanbury's work is the kind of poetry Neuburg liked – frothing with Lo!'s and O!'s, it is lush with capital-R Romanticism directed towards the natural world. But while there are often questionable moments in The Vine Press canon, *Night's Triumphs* is just ... bad. Even the oft-friendly *Occult Review* considers Hanbury's pieces to be 'artless outpourings': 'he obviously is a lover of Nature, a poet he equally obviously is not.'

So why did Victor Neuburg see fit to publish the first book of poems by the wealthy Worthing-based chief of a southeastern England brewing empire? Possibly the same reason the Sussex newspapers found *Night's Triumphs* comparable only to the likes of Wordsworth and Cowper. Printing the work of others was part of The Vine Press business model, such as it was, and with *Night's Triumphs* the household began a series of such publications that straddled the line between Neuburg's artistic interests and other motivations. By halfway through 1923, Kathleen was pregnant, so perhaps the business model seemed more important than before. It can't be said that Vine Press ever published anything completely outside its interests in eccentric anachronism and low-key decadence. But there are clues that Victor had his passions and his propositions: some later volumes were, for example, printed in far smaller numbers and seem not to have been sent to Neuburg's initial lists of potential reviewers. (Hanbury's book begins this shift: it was sent out and reviewed, if sometimes poorly (or with suspicious adoration), and was printed in an edition of 400, only slightly more modest than the more usual 550–600, but without the now-traditional de luxe versions.)

Ernest Osgood Hanbury was born into an aristocratic North Essex-based banking family, a relative of the Truman, Hanbury & Buxton group that operated London's iconic Truman brewery. Hanbury's own brewery – Jude, Hanbury & Co. – sold beer throughout Kent. Far from the 'young poet' one reviewer referred to, when *Night's Triumphs* was published its author was over 70; he died soon after, in July of 1927.

TO NATURE

O Nature! Solace and helper of woe-worn Man:
Sole support and comforter of the lonely heart:
What art thou, Spirit divine, and all beautiful?
What thy magic, by which, from note of warbling bird,
In the wind's soft murmur, and music of rippling brook,
From flowers fair, in their life and beauty joying,
From wood and field, from spreading plain and mountain's might,
From Sky lit glorious, and Ocean's vast majesty,
At sight of roseate Morn, and reddening Eve,
Or Night's fair Moon sailing in still solemnity,
And the bright mid of day, with Sun-glow gladdening,
Thou soothest the troubled soul and throbbing breast,
And stayest the o'erpent brain's restless contention?
Peace descends: in rapture heart and mind uplift,
Communing sweet with the holy calm of Nature.
O blest Mother of all! to thee I pour out my soul
In gratitude for thy tender love and sympathy:
To thee I dedicate these simple, feeble lines
With all humility and lowly reverence;
Thou, who teachest light and life and love are Man's,
And in all thy wondrous works tellest goodness.

SPRING WOODS

Come stroll in the early spring woods,
  While Nature, all bursting, is glowing;
Let us note the young year's moods,
  'Midst bush-buds and wild flowers blowing.

O'er the meadows green step quickly,
  As soft zephyr blows, and bright sun-beams;
Then from snug hollow, enclosed so thickly,
  Watch as the wood-life around us teems:

List to the hum of the busy bees;
  There, the gorgeous dragon-fly darts;
And, suddenly, as man he sees,
  Away the timid rabbit starts.

Hark! a thrush there is carolling strong
  To mate as she sits in yon thick thorn,
And from his lonely heart doth he long
  For that weary hatching-time to be gone.

Now near, now far, comes the cuckoo's call,
  Telling to us summer days are nigh;
And the lark o'erhead sings gladdest of all,
  Warbling joyous to the clear sky.

Here at our feet in wild grace bend
  The fairest flowers that Flora grows;
It needs no gardener with care to tend
  The blithe bluebell, the yellow primrose.

But how lovely their hue! how sweet their scent!
    Rather give me with them to spend my time,
Than in close greenhouse, cramped and pent,
    With costliest orchids of far-off clime.

Above, as the green boughs part and wave,
    See those peeps of spring's blue heaven –
Thanks be to the good God who gave
    Earth's loveliness, earth's trials to leaven.

O day of Spring! O day of Spring!
    Hopes renewed, and fresh joys are thine;
Nature released, thy praises doth sing;
    Herald of Summer! – Life's glad sign!

TO THE MOON

Glide on! glide! glide on!
  O Orb! in thy glowing glory!
As the oldest, sweetest story
Of man's, of woman's love
Is told again by thy lovely light:
Oh, saving, all-saving sight:
Light supreme from Heaven above:
Light of serious, sensitive love.
Shine on! shine! shine on!
Go gladness! go, O glory along!
Mingling pure pleasure with this song:
Glide on! glide! glide on!

BEFORE
THE STORM:

FOUR TALES OF OLD RUSSIA.

Before the Storm: Four Tales of Old Russia
The Princess Ouroussoff, author.
(aka Sophie de Bellegarde; aka Sofiya Urusova.)
Eve Rice, woodcut illustrations.
The Vine Press, Steyning; P.J. & A.E. Dobell, London. 1925.

The stories told by the Princess Ouroussoff in this slim and foreboding text, described by Victor Neuburg as 'fossils of an old and romantic social order' in pre-Revolution Russia, are heartfelt but with little in the way of optimism or comfort. The first story, 'The Chinese Doll', contains the lines, 'Could the loving little child rebuild what life had so mercilessly destroyed? Would she put a patch on the ugly wound and stop its smarting pain?' It's a couplet that might pass as description for the project as a whole: patching up losses with nostalgia for a time that seems difficult to remember fondly.

Princess Ouroussoff was Madame Sophie de Bellegarde, Sofiya Petrovna Urusova (1853-1928). Born to an aristocratic Russian family in Vilna or Vilnius, in what is today Lithuania, it has been suggested that she and her three sisters were the subject of the photograph that inspired Longfellow's poem, 'The Four Princesses at Wilna'. Her husband (A.V. Bellegarde) was head of the Moscow police and then Governor of Estonia before the Revolution. Her lifelong interest was in the Russian peasantry – their stories, their lives – and she appears to have been involved in philanthropy from childhood. By the time of the First World War she was already connected to London's publishing communities, translating academic historical work into English and writing a series for *The Church Times* about the lives of ordinary Russian peasants in wartime.

(While it's unlikely, I try to imagine that it is she or one of her sisters, who – as Princess Ouroussoff – knew Oscar Wilde and André Gide in the 1890s, and who famously, while hosting a dinner party one evening, shrieked as she saw a halo emerge around Wilde's head while the writer spoke.)

As Neuburg says in his introduction to *Before the Storm*, Mme. de Bellegarde lost everything in the Revolution. Her surviving brothers were shot, and she, her husband and her younger son fled into exile. (An older son had also died by the end of 1917 at the latest.) Grieving and deaf, she met the son of the Rev. Thomas Fry, the Dean of Lincoln, who recommended that she write memoirs of her pre-Revolution life as a means of distraction – which she did, for *The Church Times* and then, in the form of this book, The Vine Press. While Neuburg suggests more texts may be coming, it was not to be, and the Princess died in 1928.

Dedicated To My Son

In days of pain, in days of strife,
   I can but leave to thee I love
   The thoughts that lifted me above
The sordid cares of life.

·/.

The writer of these Tales of the Old Order in Russia lost her all in the Revolution; now, from exile, she sends out these little histories of a time that is passed away, never to return.

   As relics of an extinct age, little fossils of an old and romantic social order, these sketches are presented to the discriminating reader.

   The issue of further volumes from the same pen is contemplated in the near future.

THE PUBLISHERS.

·/.

The Marble Cross

A s I hear of each victim's end
  In a tale of the horrors of war,
No pity have I for the friend,
And I pity the wife no more
Than the fallen dead; for the wife

173

Shall find her solace, the friend forget,
But one there is, who all her life
Shall go her way with her eyelids wet:
Yea, most I pity the mother sad,
Who like a willow with weeping leaves,
Bowed with grief for the son she had,
Never forgets — forever grieves.

– NEKRASSOFF.   Tr. Basil Fry.

THE MARBLE CROSS

He only lived six years and a half. Did he have time to do any good? And he wished to do good! Like a flower which unconsciously seeks sunshine, his pure, innocent soul reflected the light and goodness of the unclouded sky it resembled. Cruel, incomprehensible death took him away, and the happy, bright child, life-loving and full of hope, was forever silenced.

Who can explain this sad enigma, who can understand it?

A white marble cross in the humble village church-yard, where he was laid to rest, alone reminds all passers-by of the sorrow of his loss. Night and day a lamp sheds its light on the small grave; like a star fallen from heaven it shines on the white cross, and has brought all around it a wonderful change. The uncared-for, seemingly forgotten graves are now tended and looked after — everywhere a loving hand is seen, flowers are planted, shrubs are cut, nettles removed, a touching desire for beauty and order appears. Why is this? Formerly a horse was allowed to feed on the grass. 'It grows here so plentifully,' said its owner, 'and no one needs it.' But that was possible only whilst the churchyard was neglected, and no one seemed to think of its beauty; now that the graves are in order this would be impossible. Life is hard in our villages, and people who are absorbed in the daily struggle for its continuance cannot give their thoughts or their time to those who are out of the strife. They have been wept over, they are prayed for, but life is for the living and not for the dead, and the care of the last resting-places of the dead ones gone before does not appeal to those who have remained behind. The higher the culture of a nation, the more prominent is that necessity of the bereaved heart.

In Italy the finest monuments of art ornament the churches and churchyards called "Campo Santo" — "The sacred field." The greatest sculptors in chiselling monuments to the memory of the dead endeavour to alleviate the grief of the mourners. All the wealth of the southern flora surrounds those monuments.

In England the peasant name of 'God's acre' testifies to this same loving care of graves. In Germany human woe has changed the churchyards into blooming gardens, where grief for the lost ones can flow unrestrained, far from the noise and turmoil of cities; only in Russia the hardness of the climate, and the still harder conditions of social life, result in an indifference which is not natural to the expansive national character.

The white cross, on the grave of the child whose smiling lips were so suddenly silenced, now spoke to everyone around and told them to remember their dead; and all listened to him — they understood his message. He told the children playing on the lawns, the merry, barefooted, strong and healthy children, to leave their games and to go in search of flowers for the bereaved mother who came every day to the grave of her beloved child. The dead boy taught a lesson of pity for human woe, and the children understood him. They left their games and ran into the woods for lilies-of-the-valley and forget-me-nots, they picked from the fields bright poppies and blue cornflowers and gave them to the bereft mother to decorate her darling's grave. Vaguely they felt her grief, and their small hands were outstretched to her with flowers, ferns, berries, and leaves — everything they could find for her.

A new force had entered into their lives, the unselfish emotion of pity had touched their hearts, and it awoke in them the recognition of a sorrow they could not understand.

Death taught them the lesson of life. Once the sorrowing mother found a bunch of ripe strawberries near the white cross, and then she understood that the child who had deprived himself of the beautiful berries for her sake had learnt a lesson of love, which would bring him its blessing. The good seed thrown into a child's receptive soul will develop into deeds of pity and kindness. Who once has felt sorrow for human grief, has looked with pity on human tears, will not pass by untouched or indifferent to suffering. His heart has been opened to recognise it, he has learnt to think of others: is that not the greatest lesson of all?

When she walked to the churchyard by a short cut through the forest she met a young shepherd, an untaught, ignorant lad, who understood her errands and brought her a bunch of wild flowers for her child's grave. Every time she went this way, she found on the same spot gathered flowers which he had put there for her. When she passed the village driving, the children ran out of almost every house to meet her; dirty, ragged, ill-clad children who stopped her carriage to give her flowers. They seemed to know that the forget-me-nots, which reminded her of the blue eyes of her little boy, and the lilies-of-the-valley which he used to gather for her, were especially dear to her, and nothing prevented these children from gathering them for her; not rain, not wind, no kind of bad weather stopped them from fulfilling their new mission of love; nothing made them forget the newly-taught lesson of unselfishness: and whoever dries a tear in Christ's name, does he not do a work of mercy?

The god of love and charity who witnessed the tears of His mother at the cross, did He not teach through his angel, the dead child, the pity that is beyond all understanding? And the children living near the churchyard who, the moment they saw her, ran towards her with the touching offerings of flowers — who taught them to understand her mood, to pity her? 'Let us go to your graves,' she used to tell them, 'your dead also would like to have flowers. Every flower laid down in love is precious, however simple it may be!'

And, when she saw that all around flowers began to grow, witnesses of loving care and thought, she understood that her child in death said what he had no time to say in life.

THE WAY
OF THE
SOUTH WIND

—

TEAMS OF
TOMORROW

The Way of the South Wind
G.D. Martineau, author.
The Vine Press, London & Steyning. 1925.

Teams of Tomorrow
G.D. Martineau, author.
Marjorie Chope, cover design.
The Vine Press, Steyning; P.J. & A.E. Dobell, London. 1926.

Gerald Durani Martineau (1897-1976) was a Captain in the Royal Sussex Regiment in the First World War as an 18-year-old, and became a schoolmaster thereafter: by the time he began publishing poetry he was in his late-twenties and yet, seemingly, retired to a life of verse and cricket, often combined. Having already done a book of Sussex landscape poems for Heffers of Cambridge in 1924, by the dawn of 1925 Neuburg had the writer's second volume – *The Way of the South Wind* – on the press. (It was in the hands of reviewers by the first week of February that year.)

This period of energy from Neuburg and the Press coincides with upheaval at Vine Cottage. Even as baby Toby was crawling around, Kathleen had begun her long-lasting affair; Vickybird, meanwhile, was spending ever-increasing amounts of time at the Sanctuary, the Utopian community a few miles over the Downs. Founded in 1923, it was there that he met and mingled with his heroes and their likeminded disciples, and renewed his passions – quite possibly having his own liaisons.

Martineau, however, was less Sanctuary material and more in the mould of another Rupert Croft-Cooke, though perhaps less ambitious. The poems in *Way of the South Wind* were what might be seen as standard Vine Press fare. Sussex landscape and legend, a bit of folksong or folksong-adjacent material, the air of the eerie and the O! Lo! Romanticism of yesteryear. His second Vine Press book, published just a year later, would launch the writer on his lifelong career with a subject less central to the Vine Press model: cricket. *Teams of Tomorrow* finds its landscape works balanced out with verse of the bat and ball, and decades later Martineau would still be singing the sport's praises.

THE IRON WATERS

A Sussex Legend.

There's iron in the pools from yeurr
As fur as Tunbridge Wells.
By Mayfield it gets sudden cleurr,
An' this is what they tells;
When Satan set 'emself to catch
Yon Saint to help 'uz game,
He found 'um justabout 'uz match,
An Dunstan wur 'uz name.
Fur, 'cordin' to old Jervey's songs,
(An' Jervey surelye knows)
Mus' Dunstan, wud 'uz red-hot tongs,
Grabs Satan by 'uz nose.
The devil tries to struggle free;
Mus' Dunstan holds 'um fast,
Until so tedious warm 'z he
He lets 'um go at last.
Wud howls Nick scrambles, runs, an' trips,
But stops at ev'ry pool,
An' there he lays 'um down an' dips
'Uz nozzle fur to cool.
An' so there's iron water yeurr;
That's how the story goes;
An' furrin' folks, 'z snuff at beer,
Gets strong on Satan's nose.

FAIRLIGHT HILL

When all is said and done,
When nothing else is new,
When all adventure's course is run
And life's long flimsy thread is spun
And hours of grace are few;
When conflict's echoes die
And strife has drunk her fill,
And earth in retrospect goes by
In dreams, how comforting to lie
Alone on Fairlight hill.

CHANCTONBURY TALES

Mark yon patch on the top there,
Lit by a gurt big moon.
Doant ye go fur to stop there,
Not if it's night nor noon.
Doan't ye go three times round it,
Not if it's clear broad day.
Satan himself, 'z crowned it,
He'll be along your way.
'Uv no doin's wud black ways;
Never no good they bring,
Sayin' the Lord's Prayer backways,
Walkin' around the Ring.
He'll be there wud a bowlful,
Brimmin' wud blackest broth,
Like fur to fill man's soul full,
Deep as the pit wud wrath.
Keep you down on the level;

Climb not there by the moon.
Them that sups wud the devil
Needs fur to stretch their spoon.

FAIRLIGHT WOODS

Softly, softly, through the fern; don't make that crashing noise:
People who are sleeping here are bad for little boys.
See those brown eyes twinkle from the hollow of a tree;
Pick your way between the roots, and follow close to me.

Scamble! Swish! A tiny rabbit – how it makes you start!
There he goes, between the trees, as bouncing as your heart.
Chirrup! Chirrup! – overhead, a sudden splash, and – look!
Something long and brown and lean is swimming in the brook.

Cross the log, and watch the water fold about the stones;
This must be what people mean by "feeling in your bones",
Feeling just as certain as the books that say they know,
England was the same just here a thousand years ago.

NOCTURNE: LYME REGIS

A jerking little point of light
Is climbing, with uncertain course,
Up, up, and up, out in the night,
Threading a pathway through the gorse.

And, as I watch the moving speck,
Pursuing still its jagged way,
With fitful flicker, swing, and check,
I ponder on that distant ray.

I muse on what the flame may show;
What features peering up the track?
How strange, this sharp desire to know
The secrets hid beyond the black!

What mortal or immortal thing
Would mount, to-night, that unseen slope?
A stranger, lost and wandering?
A lover, buoyed with burning hope?

A farmer, trudging to his rest?
A poacher of some petty kill?
What good, what evil in its quest,
The light that climbs Lyme Regis Hill?

NEWHAVEN

Why do you lie so black and harsh,
   Frowning over the ancient marsh,
Straggling under the long, green crest,
Giant toad on a gentle breast?

Here you stretch like a loathly sore,
Clamorous over the ruined shore;
West winds carry your syrens' moan
Over the hills to Bishopstone.

Marshy valley and sweeping hill,
Spray-lashed hamlet, and burnt-out mill;
These we treasure and love anew:
Only grey steamers care for you!

A MARTELLO TOWER

I climbed the rotting, wooden stair
And crossed a dark, uncertain floor,
That stirred unsafely as, with care,
Slowly I started to explore.

The musty rubbish lay, feet thick;
Each move disturbed a cloud of dust;
The plaster dropped from off the brick;
Great iron rings were red with rust.

Up narrow steps that wound aloft
A doorway framed a patch of blue,
Where, in dread days of doubting, oft
The weary watchers clattered through.

And here, recumbent, rusted, old,
Behold the giant of the tower,
A heavy mass of iron mould
That never knew an angry hour.

And by him still his mounting waits
On wheels turned brown, long starved of grease,
Robbed of war's glory by the Fates,
Dead as an argument for peace.

IN THE TREES

Old autumn's sad, becoming rust
Is shed on each dismantled bough;
While moaning comes the winter gust,
To tell the earth 'tis winter now:
  " 'Tis winter now", the dirge-like breeze
  Pipes through the world of weeping trees.

The wan old sun's receding glow
Lends but a tint to swell our grief;
He, while the bitter breezes blow,
Now glorifies a fallen leaf,
  Preaching to us, as well he can,
  A greater kindliness in man.

THE
WHITE
BLACKBIRD

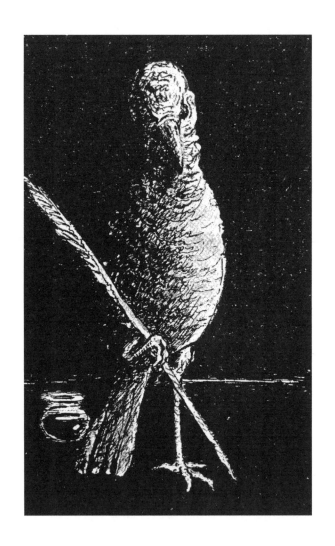

The White Blackbird
Alfred de Musset, author.
Henrietta Tayler, translated by.
Constance Tayler, illustrations.
The Vine Press, Steyning; P.J. & A.E. Dobell, London. 1927.

'Histoire d'un Merle Blanc' ('The Story of a White Blackbird') is a long-beloved satirical fable by the poet Alfred de Musset. First published in French in the 1850s, this Vine Press edition was by no means the first English-language translation – it had been in circulation on the west side of the Channel for decades by the time Neuburg began printing the novella. But it's not difficult to see why the Vickybird would be drawn to publishing such a tale: its underpinning message, of a born-outsider who finds it 'distinguished, but also inconvenient, to be a very exceptional blackbird', might as well have been gospel to Neuburg and his patchwork of counter-cultural communities.

Similarly, the Tayler sisters – translator Henrietta (c. 1870-1951) and illustrator Constance (1867-1948) – were not new to the world of letters. Henrietta, or Hetty, the younger of the two, was a historian of Scotland whose work focused on the Jacobites and, specifically, Clan Duff, from which the sisters were descended. Constance J.D. Coulson (née Tayler) had made trips to Korea around the turn of the 20th century; she wrote and illustrated two important books about Korea in a period in which such travels, particularly by women, were rare. She spent the end of her life in Arundel, west of Steyning, and may likely have already had West Sussex connections by the time *The White Blackbird* was published. Work by each Tayler sister is still used by academics in their fields today.

The White Blackbird was published in an edition of only 250 copies, with no reference to a de luxe or other special edition; the 'books received' columns in most of Neuburg's regular outlets weren't bursting with mentions. The notices it did receive were positive, with the *Eastbourne Gazette* in particular praising its subject and translation as being well-chosen for the times.

The times were, for Neuburg, the days of the Sanctuary. By the time of this book's publication, in late 1927 or even early 1928 (it is first mentioned by any press in March of that year), Neuburg was a fixture at the Sanctuary's alternative community over the Downs. He had found a miniature village full of other white blackbirds, and he intended to spend as much time with them as he could.

THE WHITE BLACKBIRD
(first section)

It is distinguished, but also inconvenient, to be a very exceptional blackbird.
I am not a fabulous bird; Monsieur Buffon describes me. But, alas, I am
very rare and hard to find. I wish I had been impossible! My father and
my mother were worthy people who lived for many years in a sheltered
old Garden in the Marais, near the Gare de l'Est in Paris. They were an
exemplary couple. While my Mother, in the depths of a thick bush, laid
her eggs regularly three times a year and hatched them drowsily in an
almost religious manner, my father, still active and irritable in spite of his
great age, hopped about around her all day, bringing lovely insects, which
he held delicately by the end of the tail, and when night fell and it was fine
he never omitted to encourage her with a song which delighted the whole
neighbourhood. There had never been a quarrel, nor the slightest cloud to
disturb this perfect union.

Almost immediately after my birth, my father began for the
first time in his life to be really cross. Although I was at that time only
a doubtful grey, my father recognised that I was not like the rest of his
numerous progeny, either in colour or appearance.

"That's a horrid child," he would say, scowling at me. "I think he must
be always rolling in plaster and mud to look so ugly and so dirty."

"Oh, my dear," my mother would reply, from the depths of an old
bowl where she had her nest, "don't you see it is only because he is young?
You yourself, were you not in your day a charming little scamp? Let our
little blackbird grow up and you will see how handsome he will be. He is
one of my finest children." But though my mother defended me thus, she
was not really deceived. She watched my fatal plumage growing and saw
that I should be a monstrosity, but, like all mothers, she was especially
fond of the child illtreated by nature, as if the fault were hers, or as if she
were anticipating and rebutting the injustice of the world towards him. At
the date of my first moult my father considered me very carefully. As long
as my feathers were still falling he was kind to me and even fed me, while I
shivered almost naked in the corner. But as soon as my poor damp wings
began to be re-covered with down, and as each white feather appeared,

he became so furious that I feared he would pull them out. Alas, I had no looking glass. I didn't know the reason and I wondered why an affectionate father should be so cruel.

One day, when the sunshine and my new feathers made me feel quite happy, in spite of myself, I was flying about and unluckily began to sing. At the first note my father sprang up as if shot. "What do I hear?" he cried. "Does a blackbird whistle like that? Do I whistle so? Is it even whistling?"

And sinking down beside my mother with a furious expression on his face, "Wretch," he cried, "Who laid an egg in your nest?" At these words my outraged mother flung herself out of the bowl, not without injuring her foot. She tried to speak, but her sobs stifled her; she fell to the ground half swooning. I thought she was dying, and, trembling with fear, I fell down before my father imploring him. "If I whistle badly, if I am badly dressed, do not punish my mother. Is it her fault if Nature has refused me a beautiful voice like yours? Is it her fault if I have not your beautiful yellow beak and your lovely black coat, which make you look like a church verger about to swallow an omelette? If Heaven has made me a monster, and if some one must bear the blame, let it be me alone."

"That is not the question," said my father. "What is that absurd way of whistling, and who taught you to do it, contrary to all rules and usage?"

"Alas, sir," I said, "I whistled as I could, feeling happy because the sun was shining and I had eaten so many flies."

"In my family one does not whistle like that," said my father furiously. "For centuries we have whistled from father to son, and I should like you to know that when my voice is heard in the evening, there is an old gentleman on the first floor, and a young girl in the attic, who open their windows to hear me. Isn't it bad enough to have before my eyes the awful colour of your silly feathers, which make you look like a dusty mattress in a fair? If I were not the most peaceful of blackbirds, I should have a hundred times ere now plucked you as bare as a chicken ready for roasting."

"If that is the case, sir," I cried, tingling at my father's injustice, "you need not trouble further; I shall remove from your sight that unlucky white tail, which you are always pulling. I shall go, sir; I shall leave you. You will have enough children to console your old age, since my mother has three families a year. I shall hide my misery far from you, and perhaps," I added sobbing, "I may find in a neighbour's garden, or on his eaves, a few worms, a few spiders with which to sustain life." "As you like," said my Father, not in the least moved by this speech. "Let me never see you again; you are *not* my son, you are *not* a blackbird." "And what am I then, sir?" "I have no idea, but not a blackbird." Having given vent to this crushing statement my father moved slowly away. My mother rose sadly and limped to her bowl, there to cry at her leisure. I, stunned and wretched, flew off as I had said, to perch upon the gutter of a neighbouring house.

My father was cruel enough to let me remain for several days in this mortifying situation. He was kind-hearted in spite of his violence, and by the way he glanced towards me occasionally I saw that he would have liked to forgive and recall me. My mother constantly raised her loving eyes towards me, and even sometimes uttered a little plaintive cry; but my horrible white plumage inspired in them such an invincible disgust that I saw it was hopeless.

I am not a blackbird, I kept on saying to myself, when performing my toilet in the morning and looking at myself in the water in the gutter. I see only too well how unlike my family I am. I wish I knew *what* I was?

One pouring wet night, I was just about to go to sleep, worn out with hunger and grief, when suddenly there alighted beside me a bird, wetter, paler, thinner than I could have believed possible. He was about my colour, as far as I could judge in the rain. He had scarcely enough feathers to cover a sparrow, and he was bigger than I. At first I thought he was a very poor and miserable bird; but in spite of the rain beating on his almost bald head, he had a certain air of pride which was altogether charming. I made a polite bow and he replied by a fierce peck which nearly knocked me off the gutter. Seeing that I pocketed the affront and merely withdrew politely without retaliation, he asked me, in a voice as hoarse as his head was bald, "Who are you?" "Alas, sir," I said, fearing a second blow, "I don't really know. I thought I was a blackbird, but I have been convinced to the contrary."

This curious answer interested him. He came nearer and made me tell him my story, which I did with all the sadness and humility suitable to my position, and to the terrible weather!

"If you were a carrier-pigeon like me," he said, "all these persecutions wouldn't worry you one bit. We travel; that is our life, and we have plenty of friends, but I don't know who my father is. Our pleasure, our very existence, is to cleave the air, traverse space, see the mountains at our feet, breathe the pure air of heaven and not the exhalations of the earth, and go like an arrow from the bow to our journey's end. I cover more ground in a day than a man does in ten."

"Indeed, sir!" I said boldly. "You are a Bohemian kind of bird."

"That doesn't trouble me," he said. "I have no country. I only care for three things – travelling, my wife, and my little ones. Where my wife is, that is my country."

"But what is that rag of paper hanging round your neck?"

"Those are important despatches," he replied, ruffling. "I am on my way to Brussels, and the news that I am taking to a celebrated Banker will cause the rate of interest to fall one franc, seventy-eight centimes."

"Dear me!" I cried. "Yours seems a fine life, and Brussels I am sure must be worth seeing. Couldn't you take me with you? As I am not a blackbird, perhaps I am a carrier pigeon."

"If you had been one," he said, "you would have pecked me back when I pecked you just now."

"Well, I will," said I. "Don't let us quarrel over such a trifle. See! the dawn is breaking and the storm is over. Do let me follow you. I have no interest in life. If you refuse, I shall drown myself in this gutter."

"All right," he said. "Let us start. Follow me if you can."

I cast one glance at the garden where my mother was sleeping, and dropped one tear. Then I spread my wings and flew away.

My wings, as I said, were not very strong yet. My guide went like the wind and I panted beside him; after a bit I became faint and giddy. "Is it much farther?" I asked feebly. "No," he said, "we are at Bourget. Only sixty leagues more." I tried to pluck up heart and not be a coward and flew on for a little longer, but all at once I was *done*. "Sir," I stammered, "could we stop for a moment? I have a terrible thirst, and if we were to perch on that tree – "

"Go to the devil. You are only a blackbird," said the furious pigeon, continuing his flight without paying any attention to me. I, blind with fatigue, fell into a corn-field and fainted. When I came to, the words "You are only a blackbird" still rang in my ears. Oh, my dear parents! I thought. You made a mistake. I will go back to you and you will know me now for your real child, and will let me have my place again in that nice heap of leaves under my mother's bowl. ...

THE STORY
OF THE
SANCTUARY

The ★ Sanctuary

1922

1932

The Story of the Sanctuary
Vera Gwendolen Pragnell, author.
The Vine Press, Steyning; P.J. & A.E. Dobell, London. 1928.

England in the 1920s was held together by hangups: politics, gender roles, sex and the body, plus, of course, James Joyce's trio of nationality, language and religion – then, as now, these nets were flung indiscriminately. The Sanctuary was founded as a way to fly past them.

Vera Pragnell was born into a family that was, as historian Rebecca Searle puts it, 'rapidly ascending the social ladder' with more-than-commensurate remuneration as well. As a teenager in London during the First World War, she worked as a nurse helping invalided soldiers; after the war, she continued in a similar vein, working in the city's slums. But the charitable organisations for which she worked were largely moralisers. Pragnell soon discovered another approach, and began to believe that the way to help people was not to damn their selves as not good enough, but to offer them opportunities for freedom. By the time she was 25, she had assembled this thinking into a framework for the Sanctuary, and in 1923 she founded the space on a plot of land acquired at the foot of the South Downs near Storrington in West Sussex.

Vickybird need only walk a few miles over his beloved Chanctonbury Ring, or take a short bus ride around it, to get from Vine Cottage to Pragnell's makeshift community of icons and hoboes; communists, proto-fascists and aging anarchists; free-thinkers and free-lovers. The eminent utopian and gay-rights advocate Edward Carpenter was both inspiration and associate; those who stayed at the Sanctuary included the likes of Laurie Lee, Dion Byngham and W.C. Owen – in its later form, Jomo Kenyatta. But for the most part, its inhabitants and guests were – as Arthur Calder-Marshall puts it – 'refugees': 'It was an asylum for almost every type of refugee, not a workshop for those who found life in the city too distracting.'

To the missionary Florence Allshorn, the Sanctuary consisted of 'mostly people who have been rather bashed about by life'. Neuburg was certainly one of those. The Quixotic poet, unable to sell books or get 'in the swim' of the literary world, was transformed whenever he crossed the Downs to the Sanctuary. There he became that most elusive beast: himself.

Pragnell met Neuburg when she needed to have some of the Sanctuary's pamphlets printed and sought out The Vine Press. By December of 1927, Neuburg was enough of a fixture at the place to have written and starred in the Sanctuary Players' pantomime show, with Pragnell, her new husband (and Edward Carpenter's former assistant and partner) Dennis Earle, the venerable anarchist W.C. Owen and other luminaries taking part. Neuburg is identified in his own programme as:

'The Very Reverend Augustus Swank Vickybird, P.I.B., M.U.G., S.A., &c., &c., Professor of Applied Tripe to the Royal University of Gotham; Exhibitioner of Bilge to His Remarkably Serene Highness the Maharajah of Tosh; Chief Examiner of Back-chat and Cross-words at Colney Hatch College; Corresponding Dog-Latin Secretary to the Cats' Home of the Persian Empire; Humgruffin-in-Ordinary to the Great Artichoke of Jerusalem, &c., &c., &c.'

That summer, around the same time that the legendary American contralto Marian Anderson was staying at Vine Cottage, Neuburg would publish Pragnell's *The Story of the Sanctuary* – still under her unmarried name, though she would soon begin using Vera Dennis Earle. It's likely that the *Story* is the book that Vickybird and Kathleen were working on when Anderson stayed. In her autobiography, the singer recalls her hosts spending most nights 'cutting the pages of books just off the press … their favorite pastime…' and describes a gleefully helpful couple going out of their way to aid her – a rather more cordial and, in fact, active partnership than described by Calder-Marshall. And why shouldn't Victor and Kathleen have been their own version of 'happy'? She had her affair, of which Neuburg was certainly aware, and he had his own: with the Sanctuary.

The sections below from The Story of the Sanctuary *include: Neuburg's poem dedicating the book to Edward Carpenter; Pragnell's original leaflet texts, as included in the book; and a lengthy passage from the main section.*

TO THE MASTER

Fitly and truly be this book to you
    Given; the seed was sown ere we were born
    By you, Master of Youth, by whom our morn
Was seen afar. All that we prize as true
Was held by you of old! Our reverence due
    Receive, O Master ever-young; be worn
    Youth's royal robes, and youth's imperial horn
Be sounded through the world: This man was true.

True through the ages! O my brave Hellene,
From age to age wearing the laurels; green
    Still be the bays for you! Be it our part
        To set the Master-heart i' the world astir!
    Love's pilgrim, sage and bard! Here's to the heart
        Of our youth's doyen, Edward Carpenter!

IV.

...Meanwhile, a little speculative leaflet was pieced together during wanderings through woods, down country lanes and over the open moors. It voiced a great hope for the future of a tract of land to be surrendered to the people. It was written in the belief that one has only to give out beautiful hints to find them greeted by a beautiful response: that the lover has but to point out his stairway to the stars and the world will follow it naturally, gratefully, gaily ...

V.

The leaflet is headed "The Sanctuary" and reads as follows: –

ORIGIN

The origin and purpose of the "Sanctuary" should be definitively stated at the outset in order to avoid otherwise inevitable misrepresentations later on.

Its origin was that call of Christ, to the individual heart, which will be found to be the basis of *any* true and deep and permanent reform.

PURPOSE

Its purpose is, purely and simply, a personal and practical application of that Christianity whose interpretation, in terms of life, alone, we maintain, holds the clue to the world's salvation.

Here, then, we have no organised movement, no new cult, no network of intricate and interesting ideas. Whatever changes or developments may come with the passage of time, the "Sanctuary" stands upon a basis which is secure inasmuch as it is a witness to the absolutely logical and spontaneous outcome of Love and the love-urge to action.

A HOUSE OF GOD

"Sanctuary Cottage" is a House of God: a workman's – e.g. craftsman's – humble dwelling dedicated to the Master-Craftsman, Christ. Hence its doors are never closed. He who comes is welcome in God's Holy Name. There are no class or "moral" distinctions, no questions asked, no rules.

RETREAT

For those who desire a period of peace and quiet and seclusion, away from the turmoil and stress of the secular world, rooms are available and no charge is made. Each is fitted up with all essentials that guests – be they men or women – can cater and cook for themselves and so ensure, should they desire it, that perfect solitude, the periodical need for which tends to grow with the increasing chaotic complexity of our present civilisation.

VOCATION

To meet the needs of any guests who may wish indefinitely to prolong a period of peace and penitence and prayer, a little Calvary-crowned hill is dedicated to those who seek to live a life mainly of solitude and that form of service which finds its best expression through contemplation, study and communion with God.

ITS CHALLENGE TO CAPITALISM

The "Sanctuary" is not owned by capitalists. No capitalist can consistently champion the cause of Christ. The converted capitalist's first concern is to surrender such means of livelihood as his capital represents. In a Christian community every living soul would have the right to claim the means of maintenance. That means, basally, is land. While land-monopoly continues there is no such thing as the "right to live"; if a man is not a capitalist he is forced to be a serf. Christianity stands as an indomitable challenge to a civilisation which is an outrage against God.

SURRENDER OF LAND

The "Sanctuary's" one-time capital is sunk in surrounding land, which is surrendered for absolutely indiscriminate distribution. In addition to the twelve half-acre arable plots (two of which go to married people) there are two acres of pasture, owned corporately, and several acres of rough, uncultivated land where settlers may build their huts around the "Sanctuary".

EDUCATION

In a Christian community every able-bodied being would support himself and education would begin, far from sophisticated class-rooms, out in the open fields. The child learns by imitation long before it learns from lesson-books. Lives that would bear the eyes of a Christ upon them would bear, also, the critical gaze of a child. *Outside* a Christian community they cannot bear the scrutiny of either, and our modern manner of living is depriving young and old of their rightful heritage and rendering parents quite unfit to teach. Hence the inevitable growth of an entirely artificial system of education which, at best, produces highly specialised beings rather than complete citizens and involves the separation of the children from the home. Its failure is everywhere apparent in the utter inability of the individual, the family or the nation to support itself and in the breakdown of a system laboriously built up by so-called "educated man".

SELF-HELP

Complete citizenship, on the other hand, entails a concentration, primarily, not upon the three R's and the mastering of some one particular trade, but upon the basal art of self-supply. Man's first necessities are love of God and access to the land. Given these for his foundation, and provided he refrains from blocking the way, those three essentials so dear to the heart of modern economists – namely, food, raiment, and shelter – are, as promised, added unto him. This does not stunt individual talent by doing away with specialisation, but it does put specialisation second to self-support. When man has mastered the means whereby he can come by simple dwelling and clothing and food, without resource to the exploitation of a single living soul, he has also made the discovery that such personal production itself provided endless scope for his energy-creative and that there is still left ample time for those three R's and the following of some particular pursuit.

SURPLUS

More: man, by the ingenuity of God, is so constructed that in a very short while he is making more than enough to meet his own needs. From that surplus, which stands for the support of those too young or ill or aged to support themselves, may be deducted sufficient to obtain that little which he needs but cannot personally produce until capitalistic monopoly of machinery gives place to the corporate manning, by the people for the people, of that little which is necessary in the really wise reordering of their lives.

SALE OR EXCHANGE

Money may be the medium of exchange employed for convenience' sake. But there is no real reason why those who fear the mischief that money's gross mishandling has made should not straightway steer for the dawn of that New Era when mutual service answering mutual need shall replace the hideous barter-haggling, and resultant High Street, system of to-day.

POOLING OF SUPER-SURPLUS SERVICE

The "Sanctuary" can but set an example; point the way to an ideal. Those who listen and watch must decide as to whether or not they will follow. For example, while each settler, unhampered by rules or restrictions, is *left entirely free to live his own life in his own way*, common sense seems to point to the pooling of all surplus over and above that little needed, through sale or exchange, for the satisfaction of needs not met by means of direct production.* Thus may be extended that Common Till the House of God should stand for: thus may the "Sanctuary" more and more become a vital centre for physical as well as psychical refreshment for the world without to draw from and – as they grow old, for instance, or are sick – the settlers themselves.

It is, too, hoped that if any claim their land and, after a while, elect to leave it, they will take toll for their labour and offer it back to the "Sanctuary" which offered it to them.

INDISCRIMINATION

Time and again the indiscriminate nature of our distribution, both within and without the "Sanctuary", causes quite considerable surprise. But we

*See Surplus.

have long since learnt that love of God leads to the doing of daring and difficult things, and any form of exclusiveness is entirely alien thereto. Men may be sinners or saints; it is not our business to judge, but rather to "give to him that asketh" and, so, to each the benefit of the doubt. We are answerable for the giving only. It is not for us, but for the recipient, to account for the treatment and the destination of the gift. Our guests' or settlers' circumstances are not our concern. Christ said, "Knock, and it shall be opened unto you". There was no preliminary demand for men's credentials and no safeguard whatever against so-called "possible abuse".

God's Kingdom upon earth is not coming through any mere provision of plots, but it cannot come until the means-of-livelihood-monopoly has ceased. Sufficient land for personal maintenance must be claimable *by all who want it,* emphatically not merely by those who are "interesting", "fine", or "deserving", in the eyes of a given few.

CHANGE OF HEART

So much, then, for external freedom. For the rest—it cannot be emphasised too strongly that true freedom is of the heart and mind. We can do no more than clear a space of quiet and calm, in the centre of the chaos of the world's activities, that each may have a chance to cultivate that spirit of true deliverance which the individual must reach out for, for himself. The "Sanctuary" – standing, as it must do to be consistently Christian, for the renunciation of capital on the part of the rich and, thus, a guarantee against starvation for the poor – does not overlook the fact that reconstruction, to be wise and real, must reach where the root of all the wrongs of the world are – that is, in the heart of man. But while a man depends upon his employer for his next meal and, hence, has no real guarantee that that meal will materialise at all,* it is not the time to appeal to his turbulent heart.

---

* The present industrial deadlock is, of course, the absolutely inevitable outcome of modern industrialism itself, doomed to occur and recur so long as the present system is in force.

And it must not be forgotten that the "Sanctuary", in standing first for the guarantee of the basal means of livelihood, gathering its settlers around it, stands, too, as it were, for a magnet in their midst: the Sanctuary-enshrined, non-exclusive and all-joyous spirit of Jesus has, throughout the ages, made man's heart its very centre of attack and is, by its very nature, divinely dynamic and very far from easy to resist.

If ever the Sacraments come to be offered here it will be at an altar at which, as at our Common Table, no living soul who seeks shall be refused.

INTELLECTUAL ACTIVITIES

We warmly welcome to the "Sanctuary" workers from all spheres of activity and lecturers in all subjects. Experience has proved that our specialising intellectual centres are crammed with men and women denied, for various reasons, that period of quiet and that "contact with all kinds" which they, especially, need so much. The "Sanctuary", with its ideal of mutual service, should thus fill a double purpose here, drawing men together on a common meeting-ground. And nowhere can men meet more absolutely freely than in the shadow of the peoples' Cross of Christ.

That is why we want (all through the length and breadth of Europe, and beyond) just such Sanctuaries where hospitality – spiritual, cultural, physical – is offered indiscriminately for the common good. Each learns from the other when the tramp as well as the "teacher" seeks the wide shelter of the House of God, whereas the spirit of learning is crushed out of all recognition when trapped in an ugly hall, whose occupants pay-at-the-door. Such gatherings, to be of value, should be perfectly spontaneous and free: a meeting round the Sanctuary fire, or on the hill-tops, in a common quest of truth.

The religious, educational and economic centre can, and must, be one beneath the banner of the Christ. And, since our civilisation is slowly starving itself to death, it is surely time for the reservoirs of the Sanctuaries of Jesus to be revealed and thrown open for the welfare of the world. We undoubtedly do need centres round which mankind may rally, each enriching the common stock with a something each other lacked. When such centres crystallise they will fly the banner of Jesus and be the true Churches of Christ.

A WARNING

Already certain sections of the community are banding themselves into little groups determined to claim their right to all uncultivated land. The number of such groups will naturally tend to increase as more and more the workers wake to the strangely simple facts of the situation; e.g., industrial freedom cannot come except by means of access to the land and if the capitalist bars the way, then, presently, the capitalist must go. Ultimate conscription of wealth is unavoidable. There must be no more luxury till everyone is guaranteed the necessities of life. That is the cry of Labour, though, when it reaches us only by means of a capitalist Press, it is not easy to interpret or in any way to associate it with, two thousand years ago, the cry, also, of Christ.

Then if this thing is coming, anyway . . .?

The "Sanctuary" stands for love *versus* a not improbable alternative basis of fear.

It recognises the fact that it is a case of conversion to-day or, alternatively, confiscation to-morrow. If confiscation is the basis of the new World Order it will probably prove but little saner, sounder or more peaceful than the old.

Therefore we cannot stress the point too strongly that "God's good time", undoubtedly, is *now*.

The "Sanctuary" must stand for a practical demonstration of the fact that only a turning (not returning – it has never yet been given a chance) to the teaching and spirit of Jesus can really make the basis of society secure. Anyone can play an accompaniment; what the world wants is *someone to lead the dance!*

But, at the same time, it would enlist the support of every preacher, speaker, teacher, writer . . . in the land, in a great campaign to prove the practicability of the economics of Jesus and with a view to setting up other

"Sanctuaries" in other counties and other lands that, growing up as the present system steadily breaks down, they may be there to answer the needs of the masses as befits the Houses of God.

VI.

At last the land was discovered at the foot of the South Downs: a beautiful tract of about 19 acres of common, eight acres of arable land, a lovely heather-covered, sentinel-like hill and two semi-detached, derelict cottages. It was near enough to the main road to be reasonably accessible, far enough from it to feel delightfully shut away from the merely curious. *And* there were no building restrictions! The missing details as to acreage, etc., were filled in, in the leaflet, as given, the Haslemere cottage was disposed of and these very humble dwellings with the surrounding lovely land were taken on.

Shortly before Christmas, 1923, my worldly goods, my donkey and I moved to Storrington. Until the cottage was habitable I lived in a small caravan which rocked about, on windy nights, like a ship at sea. In those wintry days our common was an exquisitely lonely spot but the donkey and I had a morbid love of desolate places and we were boundlessly happy. Someone says somewhere that "in the wilderness and the solitary places God speaks to the heart of man" – I am quite sure he spoke to ours. Everything seemed pregnant with heavenly meaning and possibilities and, continually conscious of the presence of the divine lover, it was natural enough to do "all to the glory of God".

There was much to be done. Six acres of arable land were staked out in half-acre allotments and the remaining two were railed off into two grass plots, one of which is now used for a children's playground and camping pitch. The cottages were knocked into one and were put into order that the earliest settlers might reside and feed there, if they wished, whilst erecting some sort of shacks for themselves. And on the hill-top a very beautiful Calvary was erected. The crucifix was carved by a Belgian whose love of God is reflected in his work. It serves many purposes. Primarily, it is there to declare to the world in general and to those who settle on Sanctuary land the reason why that land was freed. At the same time it acts, I think, as a reminder to some of us, that the crucifixion is no mere event in history but is perpetuated in our lives – inasmuch as we support a civilisation in which Beauty is very definitely on a cross. Hence it may act, sometimes, as a deterrent . . . . who shall say? If that is too sanguine, well – at least it can be claimed for it that sometimes someone looks up at the exquisite, challenging thing. And that, surely, is all to the good. "Whatsoever is lovely", quoth the poet, "*Dwell on these things.*"

The heath-covered hill which the crucifix surmounts is still unpeopled. Perhaps all the true contemplatives have sought the protection of the cloister with the solace of the Sacraments and the safe-guard of a written rule of life. Anyway it is peaceful and beautiful and there at least the bunnies are unmolested and the harmless grass-snakes wriggle out into the sunshine free from the wrath of hysterical humans for once.

From the hill-top one can see Cowfold's vast Carthusian Monastery, where the white-habited friars so beautifully combine manual work and contemplation, living a life of solitude-in-community which fills the heart with wonder and thanksgiving in this so-called practical world. Moreover, when a kind wind blows in the right direction one can hear the bells of another monastery whose kindly Prior came willingly to bless Calvary-Hill, the cottage, the land and non-Churchman me!

Christmas was wonderful. I seldom enter churches and have come to use the term *Christianity* very warily and seldom, so far removed seem Churches and Christianities from the daring spirit of Christ. But on Christmas Eve I went to the Monastery's Midnight Mass and knelt at the Cradle of the Holy Child and, coming home, got completely and utterly lost! Never, surely, was a lost thing happier than I: the Mass music rang in my ears, haunting and beautiful, and the night was deliciously frosty and pitch dark. The cold wind blew in my face, defying sleepiness, and every now and again a frightened bird would fly up, screeching, as I plodded on, up hill and down dale, my foot slipping into bunny-holes, my arms striking against trees. Once, it was the howl of a fox that broke the silence of that amazing night. And never a sign of a dwelling and not one guiding star! Towards dawn I came to a cottage and its red-bearded cowman-owner insisted on accompanying me all the way back, many miles, to my caravan-home.

"You seemed such a chit of a child", he said gently, "and my girl's across the Sea and I'd like to think someone would do the same for her."

So we drank hot cocoa in the van and he tucked me up with clumsy tenderness as we wished each other Happy Christmasses.

VII.

Gradually it became known, mainly through the medium of a little paper to which I was a regular contributor, that a small tract of land was being freed. People claimed plots for very various reasons and references were, of course, not required. One man volunteered his, writing from the north of England, that access to the land would be as the way to the Holy City, for him, and that in the wilderness, if anywhere, he would find God. Some came for quite material reasons, of course, and a very few, naturally desiring recognised security, asked for legal ownership of their plots, which was readily granted – provided they paid the expenses of any legal transaction. Those who wished to keep their land for cultivation, only, built their little shacks on the common where several others – anxious to live with us although the plots were by then all claimed – have, from time to time, added their little dwellings. But, please note our family has really reached its limits now!

The actual Sanctuary differs from the original leaflet in that: (1) The whole of Sanctuary Cottage is now placed freely at the disposal of guests during the summer months, for I move into it for the winter only (if ever). (2) It is no longer technically correct to say "The Sanctuary is not owned by capitalists", since I, its legal owner, have a very minute income and although it has to be substantially supplemented by hard work – well, there it is! And there it will remain so long as the outer world – *via* letters and visitations – continues to make such immense demands on my time. Meanwhile we can but strive to give in service at least as much as we receive in cash. (3) There has been no serious (corporate) effort towards exchange in place of barter or towards the extension of a common pool. Both have to some extent been practiced by two different groups of friends – successfully, I think, perhaps because they were a natural outcome of deep affection and trust.

From what immensely different angles different people view the same thing! A young man to whom I was talking a few weeks ago suddenly spoke of The Sanctuary, where he had camped for several weeks. "Lord! The heavenly possibilities of the blessed spot!" he said, "and you have one or two *beautiful* people." Another called at my hut on the same day. "Why do you live here?" he asked. "What will you ever accomplish with, for the most part, a handful of gossiping women and futile men?" One thought of the two who looked through prison bars ("the one saw mud; the other – stars").

I am not, of course, trying to accomplish *anything – for others*. I have long since ceased to dream dreams for people who are, I have no reason to doubt, quite capable of dreaming for themselves. Probably it is harder, worthier and wiser to go quietly on, attending to one's personal contribution: that is, continually *endeavouring to be true*, living out the joyous counsels of the secret, still small voice; expressing one's inner ecstasy fearlessly, merrily, in one's individual life. "That's the idea", but heaven knows it is not always easy. Every now and again when in the midst of what my future husband wantonly and quite inaccurately terms "good works", some wretched thing within me queries. "Is he (or she) *worth* it?" And I am forced to make mighty efforts to recapture something of the old, adventurous spirit which would make haste to answer – "Goodness yes: *It may be Christ!*" Sometimes the disguise seems inches thick.

When first working in the slums I used to think what a lovely thing men might make of life, given land to build on and freedom to build (using the word in its widest possible sense) what they pleased: given, that is, the barest *chance* that that essentially involves *despite* the enormous difficulties, to-day, of wresting a decent livelihood from the land. But, alas, we have wandered too far from simple living and wise values and the vision of God. With the advance of civilisation, grotesque in its greed and callousness and in its worship of complexity and speed, our finer senses have become numbed; our vision dulled and our wants so many that, ironically, and paradoxically, man can move nearer his idea of satisfaction only by means of that vast economic machinery which is his worst enemy. Apropos, several have come to us, believing they want freedom, only to find it is the hardest thing on earth to cope with, in the self-mastery it involves. And so they have slipped quietly back – almost eagerly – to slavery again. Have we been for too long divorced from freedom and from the soil to make very much, given both, of either? The pathos of it all!

WOT'S THE GAME:

ENGLAND'S POST-WAR BOOK.

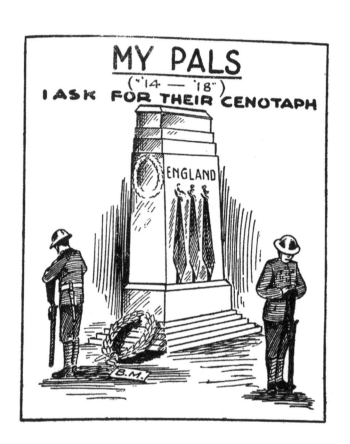

Wot's the Game: England's Post-War Book
Ex-Private Billy Muggins, author.
(Possibly Victor Neuburg, pseud.)
(Illustrations uncredited.)
The Vine Press, Steyning. 1928.

Victor Neuburg's experience during the First World War was limited in time and scope, but not in impact. While his ineptitude as a soldier was equalled only by his disinterest in war, there was perhaps more military spirit of camaraderie than one might expect of the countercultural eccentric, as illustrated by his lifelong singing of army songs and the friendships that stuck with him long after. But by 1928, with Europe already descending into its various states of nationalism, the macho leer of post-war England had grated on him for too long. Friendships with conscientious objectors and anarchists such as H.D. Jennings 'Rold' White and W.C. Owen had become the norm, and his involvement with the newly formed Labour party – in a Tory stronghold such as Steyning, no less – put him at odds with an increasing nationalist strongman-anxiety prevalent in publications such as *John Bull*.

Wot's *The Game* is a unique piece in the Vine Press bibliography. It is at its heart a series of satirical political cartoons in the style of *John Bull* magazine, and accompanying pieces of writing that are, by turns, indecipherable to the 21st-century reader and entirely of the 2020s moment. 'Billy Muggins' writes in occasionally slurred speech and the dropped-'H', familiar as derogatory mockney slang, but his knowledge of the *John Bull* way of thinking comes from a lived experience among soldiers and surrounded by their post-war thinking.

There is little doubt that inspiration for the book comes in part from a pamphlet by one 'Thomas Atkins' (like Billy Muggins, slang for the common British soldier), the wonderfully titled 'Reign of Erficial Ekkernomic Terrer, 1928. Magner Cartoss. "On the economic position of England"'. But even with its similarly wanton use of spelling and mockney, Wot's *The Game* is hard to pin down: its over-the-top pro-business, anti-bureaucracy message may be satirical, but it also seems occasionally sympathetic to the capitalist cause. Any 1928 hardliner – business or union, Tory or Labour, macho soldier or fey poet – could find pages to cut out and pin to their wall.

Whether or not Neuburg wrote the whole of *Wot's The Game* remains up for grabs. As does the origin of its illustrations: are they newly created, or taken from a different context and repurposed? The book certainly plays with contemporary conventions – there are pages emulating specific magazines including *Punch* and *John Bull* in form and type, while others act like poetry chapbooks. I haven't found evidence of these specific images appearing in other publications first; that Neuburg was clipping, repasting and re-contextualising found images. But it's a tantalising – if unlikely – possibility to think that they are just such an act of bricolage.

But he was certainly behind large sections of it. Linguistic clues such as the book's use of Neuburgian acronyms ('P.W.D.' for Post-War Difficulties), its ironic quoting of Rupert Brooke and the long-winded titles and names reminiscent of Neuburg's own self-references show his hand. And it's in the 'Apologue' poem that we begin to see the Neuburg of *Comment* magazine, just a few years down the line. Its satire is more direct – a punk-poet like John Cooper Clarke or Attila the Stockbroker could do it justice – and the references to camels and to loving 'the beast' just might be allusions to Neuburg's own life.

But beyond satire and humour, post-modern mash-ups and poetic ramblings, the most likely explanation for this outlier in the Vine Press list is Neuburg's own political attitudes, which were being recharged by his new Sanctuary associations. Vickybird's friendship with W.C. Owen had blossomed to the point that the family referred to him as 'Uncle Owen', and in 1926 the elderly radical wrote to friends that he had 'stirred [Neuburg] up, as also his wife' in terms of anarchist politics. Neuburg felt, according to Owen, that 'nothing can save this situation' in mid-'20s England. In the wake of the 1926 general strike, Neuburg was moving, as his granddaughter Caroline Robertson has written, 'from passive to active support of anarchism', and – as small a step as *Wot's The Game* might be – it may have been a game-changer for the poet.

APOLOGUE

To prevent the slightest suggestion that my reputation as a soldier
was insufficient for me to publish this monumental work in praise of
Officialdom, Lethargy, and Bunkum; I present my record herewith,
which, I suggest, is second to none.

Muggins is my name,
I'm far from being clever;
To dodge from being brave
Was always my endeavour.
In finding better 'oles
I daily grew more skilled;
(How *could* we win a war
If all our side got killed?)
They got a camel naughty,
And gave it me, out East;
I say it wasn't sporty;
I didn't *love* the beast.
And then they fought poor Abdul,
(I'm sure no Christians orter),
And said to me, "You iggery*,
And fire that blinking mortar."
Now Engineerin' ain't my line;
How *could* I help their swears?
On addin' up, I now opine
I killed *our'n* more than *theirs*;
And then they thought they'd finish me,
And send me off to Heaven;

* Egyptian for 'hurry'.

And told me I must mend my ways,
And learn a three point seven.*
Still many victories did I win
Amid the war of nations;
Ere each "inspection day" had dawned
I'd won my mate's iron rations.
I wasn't, no! I wasn't brave,
I didn't do things suddin';
I'm not a V.C.-hunting slave;
(I *scorn* their Christmas Puddin').
I think that wars are *rotten* things,
In fact I thought them wicket;
The only thing I wanted to
I won, and that's *my ticket*.
I never was a soldier bold,
In love with war's bad habits;
I'm jolly glad to be back home,
So's I can feed my rabbits.

* A famous mortar, quite safe to the enemy.

SEVEN YEARS

THE HERMES BOOKS:

NUMBER ONE

Seven Years
The Hermes Books: Number One
Shirley Tarn, author.
The Vine Press, London & Steyning. 1928.

In 1928, Neuburg tried a new tack with The Vine Press, for a new author – or at least a new name – and in doing so created a tiny literary mystery. Shirley Tarn's book of sonnets, *Seven Years*, is published in an inexpensive and relatively simple manner through a new imprint the publisher calls the Hermes Books. The idea was to appeal to 'readers' rather than 'collectors' by making books that are still limited editions but at a lower price point. (That Vine Press books had trouble selling because of their cost seems unlikely – the earlier prices were comparable to, and in some cases were already below, the going rates.) *Seven Years* as a concept predates the Hermes Books idea: it is mentioned as early as February of 1925, at which point it was boosted as being 'in preparation' in promotional materials. (The same promos also tout *Before the Storm*, which would be published in 1925; yet *Seven Years* wouldn't appear until late 1928.)

But the mystery lies in the identity of 'Shirley Tarn': we don't know anything about them. There are a few clues. Jean Overton Fuller believes the name to be a pseudonym of Victor Neuburg's, and I believe that to be at least a possibility, but an unlikely one. While she has made some astute observations, Fuller's reasons are circumstantial, and her similar guesswork with Rold White (see next section) tarnishes her pseud-spotting rep. Tarn uses the word 'aureate', one of Vickybird's 'special words' that he had used in previous work he showed Fuller; Tarn references the desert, and Fuller finds echoes of James Thomson's poem 'Cities of Dreadful Night', a piece which Neuburg adored, in *Seven Years*. The publisher's relationship with Crowley had lasted seven years, and there is language throughout the poems that is of a piece with Neuburg's descriptions of the Beast.

It is also true that the name 'Shirley Tarn' doesn't appear in any birth, death or residency records that would coincide with that period; that *Seven Years* notes Tarn as being of Sussex, which might reference

Neuburg as well; and that the British Library's copy is signed by 'Shirley Tarn' in letters suspiciously similar to Neuburg's writing, if somewhat staged and careful. Other copies appear to be signed by Neuburg – one copy referred to in a bibliography is signed *to* Shirley Tarn; the copy held by Buffalo, New York's famed poetry library, is signed by Neuburg to the poet Wilfred Rowland Childe – a full-page signature 'with the publisher's best wishes'.

But there are significant reasons to doubt Neuburg as the author, notably that the same promotional materials that give notice of *Seven Years* as being 'in preparation' mention in the same section that 'All Victor B. Neuburg's unpublished works' are similarly coming soon. Why use a pseudonym alongside multiple instances of his own name? And most importantly of all, there is Rold White, whom Fuller also suspected of being a Neuburg pseudonym. White was very much an individual, and in his refutation of Fuller's suspicions, recalled conversations with Neuburg about the high quality of work by one 'Shirley Tarn'.

Could it be that the Hermes Press's other author, Ethel Archer (see *Phantasy*), had written these works, of the seven years since the wartime death of her husband? Or that Runia MacLeod, whose many, many names we will come to later, published her poetry in this guise? It's most likely, of course, that there was a man or woman named or going by Shirley Tarn living in Sussex in the 1920s; one who has escaped most of history's records. (A revelation in the 1921 census is also possible, once that becomes public.) Or that it is a *nom de plume* for someone else of little or no repute; someone too shy to participate in any literary world, who simply handed their work to their friend Victor Neuburg to produce as he saw fit.

I propose another way of viewing these works: to imagine the origin of these poems as being The Vine Press itself. It is an amalgamation of this strange family's works – the crumbling psyche of Victor Benjamin Neuburg; the still-shattered heart of Ethel Archer or of Princess Ouroussoff; the lost and broken souls of the Sanctuary; the yearning, trapped life of Runia MacLeod. The *Seven Years* sonnets are cries each would recognise; a body that each could call their own.

Seven Years is reproduced here in full.

THE HERMES BOOKS:
NUMBER ONE

A HIGH NOTE

This little volume, the first of THE HERMES BOOKS, is a challenge.

That books are primarily for readers, rather than for 'collectors', is a fact that is becoming overlooked in an age that produces cheaply and mechanically for readers on the one hand, and expensively and uncomfortably for 'collectors' on the other.

This present volume is an attempt to give true book-lovers a hand-set, individualised book at a price within the reach of all who love, and desire to possess, beauty. So much for the *format*; the content will speak for itself, and so needs no word of commendation here. All future volumes of the Series will be of a high literary standard.

The success of these books must depend upon their reception by the book-lovers and art-lovers of this country and America. We hope to produce many volumes in the present *format*.

V.B.N.

SEVEN YEARS

"Sir, you have wrestled well, and overthrown
More than your enemies."

I.

B ELOVED, the sun has waved a wand of gold,
And changed my tresses to a burnished net
Meet for a royal robe; its shining fret
A sanctuary keeps where kings might fold.
Beloved, the sun has fired my heart ... Behold!
Beyond my lawn a great red rose has met
And softly kissed a trembling weed, tear-wet,
A humble lonely star upon the mould.

O laggard years! How many cruel suns
Shall burn my heart and wake the glowing rose
To mock my lonely grief? When shall I fear
The sun and the rose no more? O mocking ones,
In pity tell, which year shall bring repose?
Beloved, see, the sun has crept too near!

2.

H OW swiftly on the fierce volcanic verge
Their golden interlude the wise folk seize,
Full knowing how, their anguish to appease,
Close on majestic wrathfulness shall 'merge
Bounty from that same hand that erst did scourge;
Full knowing days of woe yield days of ease.
Oh they were fools to waste upon their knees
The fleet good hours in vain lament or dirge!

So I, Beloved, haste back about thy ways,
And gather wealth from thy great heart's remorse,
Who for each hurt a royal gift will give,
For every overshadowed hour, sunblaze.
Let devastation follow in its course,
To-day, before thy courts I laugh and live!

3.

BELOVED! If we two lived in the days
Of good King Solomon, and thou wert king,
Too well I know, still at thy gates I'd sing
Unheeded in the desert dust thy praise;
And faint still in thy proud unseeing gaze;
And cry in vain to thee my hunger's sting;
And still my desert flowers despisèd fling
Beneath thy wheels; and still would haunt thy ways!

So haply for my meed, thy mettled steeds
My prisoned soul should from the dust unbar,
In hidden majesty henceforth to ride,
With whispered chaunts, and all my desert weeds
In ghostly bloom, and thou who wert so far,
Glowing, unknowing, by thy closest bride.

4.

HIDES haply here some secret glamoured rune,
Unwist among my people of the tent,
For gain before thy portal shall present
Thee, jewelled city's gem, my journey's boon.
How tediously, in vain, I won the tune
Of thy melodious tongue; how vainly blent
Tears, desert wiles, and arts thy people lent;
Vain, on the lintel, raged my heart's simoon!

Beloved Greek, without thy city gate,
A little space, prone in the desert dust,
Silent and very patiently I lie.
The sands slip through my hands; so still I wait.
The great sun comes and goes; I wait and trust.
I shall learn how to lure thee ere I die!

5.

DEAR perjured churl, thy newly pictured face
New-lifts the scorned percipience of mine eyes.
In piercing beauty here thy semblance lies,
Unscreened for scrutiny; each royal grace
From Nature's noblest mood; each delicate trace
Of Time, thy lover's, passionate artistries;
And light that heals, sanctions and sanctifies,
From out thy soul's inviolate hiding place.

If I have erred, who flung my heart to thee
To be thy foot-stool, Nature was my cheat,
Who built thee kingly, homage to command;
If I am mad, then Time consorts with me,
And joyously we clasp our rich deceit,
And if we could, we would not understand.

6.
A.

BELOVED, they lie not in the dark alone,
Though cold and scattered my lost nearling seem;
They dwell where tenderness holds them supreme…
The heedless beauty-hungered sire, who won
Joy, finger-tossed, from a baby's saffron crown;
The sister child, adrift her ardent stream

Of colour and line; and he that from my dream
Called me to life; and my little laughing son.

Beloved, no; they lie not in the dark;
And if through my warm heart, their ingle, drift
One mistral memory, with a hasty hand
Draw I rich curtains, stir a brighter spark
In the fire's glow .... Oh would I knew such shrift
Were mine from thee, were I in that wan band!

7.
B.

I HAVE begotten thee from out thy fane
Of dreaming thought, and with proud fingers touch
And boast thy beauty. Thy sister, I, o'ermuch
Given to love perfection, thee. Again,
I am ruthless life, wakening thee to pain.
I am thy laughing child, thy travail's crutch,
Thine armour from despair, whose loving clutch
Defiant would bar thy high meridian's wane.

Oh that gentle death would stoop to me,
And hide away from thee my every fault
That irked or hurt thee! Oh that he would come
And carry me, fair robed and crowned, to thee,
And lay me consecrate in that proud vault
Thy soul, new lit and warmed, sanctuary, home!

8.

TIRE me not yet in pearly cerements,
Nor cross my hands quiescent upon my heart
Enfolding faint fair lilies; nor yet impart

The pale appraise of thine impenitence
With glimmering candle-light. Admonishments
Efface not yet with dulcet counterpart
Of clemency. I lie not yet to court
Nor meekly claim thy pitying reverence.

I will flaunt in royal purple ere the white
Encompass me, Beloved, and mine embrace
With more than waxen blossoms shall heal thy brand;
And thou and I exultingly will light
Red flambeaux round thy pride's dark burial place,
And mine, not thine, shall be the pardoning hand!

9.

SILENCE? Nay, how shall traitrous Silence rede
This desperate argument betwixt us twain?
Shall Silence cozen me of years again?
Shall these, my early silvered tresses plead
For his ascent? Or these deep wounds that bleed
Yet from the prison stones? Or the echoing strain
Of his mocking mirth me similingly regain
Back to the living tomb that you decreed?

'Twas Silence, thy chief torturer, who piled
High the great wall on me and bitter cold,
Gaunt dark, and hunger grim, while in my stead
A puppet me thy dreaming hours beguiled,
A pretty trifling thing, rose-pink and gold ...
Silence shall win, Beloved, when I am dead!

10.

BELOVED thou shalt not fashion thee a toy
From my encruciate soul! I will not be
A glamourous wine for sensuous hours to thee;
A silken threnody 'neath the throstle's joy!
See not in me an exquisite alloy
On autumn's silver gossamer, cast free,
And floating mistily forlorn, nor see
A faery wrack thy lone fire's plash convoy.

Not for this delicate boon my bitter siege
Upon that grim old granite rock, thy soul;
No dainty murmurous shell I, to implore
A niche on thy dark surface. Loose thy rage!
Hate, strike, repel! Nay, fling me from my goal!
I shall return and rive thee to thy core!

11.

WHAT? Love me a little for my merit's sake;
A spectral far-off guerdon if I am mute
Through pain's perpetuity? Doth this innocence suit
Beloved, thy grave years? I cry thee wake!
Go forth and see unpilloried plunderers take
Rich jewelled hearts immune. If love's salute
Be worth's alone, how throng the destitute!
Nay, who so fallen this feast may not partake?

Love I not thee, immutably, though far
From chivalry's fair field this frantic strife
Has thrown thee? Though the Voice on my shamed breath
Thee wrought my tremulous pride to tread and mar,
Though thou hast slain my smile in anger rife,
I love thee, kind or cruel, unto death.

12.

AYE, let us now be done with courtesies.
A silken livery but scantly gears
The uncivil hurricance's plaything. Seven years
Has thou amerced my shamed apologies,
And ceded suave reprise, thine amnesties;
And close on each new treaty's heel appears
Resurgence. Come, 'tis time to strip thy fears,
And prink no more in mannered mummeries.

Silk shall not serve thee more than linkëd mail;
Dies gentle law before a Titan's gage.
Oh see the brimming river wreck the vale!
Oh hear the skies a-crash on the storm's rage!
Oh see the cast-away broken upon the rock!
And me no more with thy forgiveness mock!

13.

NAY Brother, I will gird at thee no more
For this mischance upon our strange lone way
From Dark to Dark. No more I'll grieve nor pray;
Out spent am I. The Eyes may leer, abhor,
Or weep; 'tis one. Now let the Hand that bore
The Phial to my lips and me to stray
Thee-ward, be clawed, divine, or frenzied clay
In Beauty's thrall ... I cannot learn this lore.

Pass on thy way then, Brother, since thou must,
And leave me broken, stripped, on these rough stones
The Hand spread for my bed. Lo! on my shame
Unstricken travellers spit; cry, "Here's foul Lust,
Vanquished!" And from the Dark no Voice atones,
Nor Light illumes the enigma of this game.

14.

COMES night with banneret flare and prismic fire,
And aureate jet and sphere. Athwart the gloom
The Carnival sweeps on. By his resting loom
Slumbers tired Thought. And bold o'er mead, o'er mire,
Gaily companioned, goes each heedless squire...
Pontiff and Prince and Courtier; Clown and Groom,
Fool and Knave and Satyr and Slave, full room
For all about the festival of Desire.

Across the throng to me thy beauty thunders,
Thou gravely pondering majesty of thy race;
And yonder grinning old Silenus blunders,
Interleaving hiccough with bloat embrace;
And thy clear lamp shall soon from thee be wrenched,
And my fair torch lie shattered, trampled, quenched.

15.

SHALL I, Beloved, now thy lesson apply
Where I a sylvan kingdom proudly rule,
Fair absent summer's regent? Dost thou school
That I arraign this growth that scans the sky
Dauntless; whose sinuous roots, earth-clinging, lie
Deepest and widest; this yearly spinning spool
Of rich magnificence; this warrantied tool
Of bounty; is it this flower that must die?

Then deeper yet thy mystic wisdom score;
So, when the pyre is strewn, the regenerate space
More lowly given: when busy zealots once more
On buzzing embassies find a paler grace,
May I extenuate my garden's dearth.
Beloved, say ... who shall inherit the earth?

16.

COME, let us now fling down the fairest tower
That boasts man's prowess from the highest hill:
And let us now the Wine of Wines be-spill
Upon the pervious earth. The paragon flower
Of every garden slay. From every bower,
From temple, forum, palace, lead forth and kill
The noblest. Richest fallow never till.
Dost thou not teach, Beloved, "Thus said the Sower"?

Oh thou who art so sore concerned for man,
Frustrate and mocked; strong-pinioned soul a-beat
Tireless upon the spheres and 'thwart the span
Of ripening young Time, now I entreat,
Unveil this mystery, how strength's effacement
Shall end the tedious night of man's abasement.

17.

STERN visaged Knight, riding alone, afar
From thy bleak fastness, upon the tourney's call,
In steely mail, gray-mantled, winning all
Thy thousand victories with never a scar,
Nor flush, nor smile ... here where the garlands are,
And beating hearts, quick blood may rise and fall,
And hidden tears, for thee; for over brawl
And trumpetry, thy silence hangs, a star.

Thy victory gained, so grimly forth alone
Ridest thou, with never a backward glance,
And never a thought for gentler wars unwon
And never a sigh upon a rusting lance.
Stern visaged Knight, niggard of glance and breath,
Is thy dark secret love old haggard Death?

18.

Is this The Lady Sin strays here alone?
Methought The Lady Sin could ne'er display
So wan a face; nor yet so tattered stray
Ungarlanded. Here is no scarlet gown,
Nor golden shoon, nor minstrelsy, nor strown
Roses about her feet; nor dazzling ray
Of jewelling upon her. Upon this way
Nor feast nor laughter. Even the skies here frown.

And see, upon the wanderer's frozen breast
Shines aught, not jewelled, in the winter sun;
Not petalled crimson flecks the pathway pressed
By naked feet; and as she trails forlorn,
Rise sounds too drear for lyre or mandolin.
I cannot think this be The Lady Sin.

19.

YOUNG laughing Time grows weary of his toys,
And thriftily fairest plaything puts to use.
Thus ever his wont, who yearly doth unloose
The pretty gauds of spring, nor yet destroys,
Ere he turn to summer's game, but straight employs
His stale delight earth's bounty to seduce.
Thou dost grave wrong, Beloved, with thy misuse
Of doubt on this most provident of boys.

Even this Wheel of Flame, this Fiery Zone
Inflexuous, this Scintillate Hoop, impune
In dizzy recklessness, a-roll, unthrown,
For Thought's long wearihood, may bear some boon
Preludious. Young time, some virile day,
May straighten this bauble to luminate our way.

20.

WOE to ye, watchers by the Temple gate,
Who watch and wait unsatisfied so long;
Who chaunt in vain, or cry upon the wrong
Of wasted tears and spilth of years; who wait
The unbeginning Sacrifice in state,
Crownëd and purple robed and fair. Along
This way he yet may pass, but woe for song,
And woe for hunger his coming shall not sate!

He will pass by alone to seek the Grail
In strange far lands; or haply to a dim
Cold hiddenness, high-walled, alone to wail
An unregenerate world. Raise not to him
Thy hands, nor grasp his mantle in thy fears,
He will but leave it there to catch thy tears.

21.

NOW roaring flame unto the furnace bear;
With leaping wave the water's turbulence 'suage;
Cry the wild skies to meet the whirlwind's rage
With howling blast and hurricane. Now declare
Pestilence the physician of famine; square
Locust and murrain, frog and hail; now 'gage
Two woes, where death's victorious cortège
Enarms decay's for healing fell despair.

Nay, bring me no fantastic crown, 'tis thine,
Thine, Renegade, if this wild lore of love
Be mad as I do think it. Seek for mine
In thy philosophy that did reprove
My early sad unfaith. Aspiring man,
Taught thou, has risen since this strange world began.

22.

NOW heart be still, for see unto the west
Hath trodden he the tumult of thine urge
In regal splendour; see, he doth emerge
Beyond thy veiling woe, and throned doth rest
Where opalescent blazonries manifest
His realm's expanse, and radiantly converge.
Oh quiet, soul! See rose and purple surge,
And jasper seas and sapphire leash thy quest.

Oh quiet, soul! Serene be in his sight;
Nor dare with grief his evensong to mar;
Nor fear thou, for his fire has changed to light,
And vigilantly he journeyed, high and far.
Now kingly will he send, with war's surcease,
From his great treasury, glowing cloths of peace.

23.

SIR Knight, if life were yet our dainty feast
Untasted, or a melody in store
With viols attuned; if eager feet before
The shimmering wistful uplands lay; if east
Lay nought but morning pleasaunces, new-leased
And lightly left, then blithely on Time's shore
With thy stern tumult should my pebbles war
In dancing hardihood and valiant jest.

But now the feast has staled; the viols were tuned
But minorly; the crags grow bleak; the rear
Stalks darkly close with spectral prescience booned
And fraught before us lies one step most clear.
O weary Knight, reach me thy hand again,
Lest thou or I live haunted with new pain.

24.

SHALL I, if sober evening creep my way,
Light's magic green mistily to conceal
That now delights me: and if silence steal
Upon mine ears, where melody all day
Dear ecstacy chimes home – shall I bewray
My present joy, and traitrously repeal
My morning psalm, and noontide praise congeal
With self-excusing smiles, ... and faith gainsay?

Oh chill are twilight folk, and dim their eyes,
And faint their voices, and their memories nod;
Their steps are slow, and they are very wise. ...
No man hath walked, prate they, so like a god
As I be-paint my love. Am I then won? ....
The soul of my belovëd mocks the sun!

25.

THE city of my lord hath ramparts high,
Of gold-wreathed alabaster, featly wrought
In gracious ornature; a thrice-armed fort
Where splendour, beauty, and bright lances vie
Defiantly. About his gateway lie,
Like sombre ships upon a moon-gilt port,
Five ebon giants, who may not be bought.
The city of my lord be-scales the sky.

Within are vales and clambering wealds, ablaze
With odorous hue, and lilied lakes, and brooks
That laugh unto the sun, and winding ways
Melodious, and secret shadowy nooks,
And stately galleries, and tapised stairs,
And sheening spires that crest the heavenly airs.

NEVER more, beyond the crest of the star-sown firmament,
Shall soar a joyous shade the luminous wold,
Hearkening in molten unison silver chimings,
Ringing a sweet dark muted secret love they told.

Nevermore when April melody steals disquieting,
Never more when the troublous blossoms of May blow free,
Never more through the scented sounds and visions of June,
Shall wing my sweet dark muted secret love to thee.

What shall I do now with all my days
Who wove the golden thread of thee
In and out through every shining hour?
And what shall I do now with the long lone nights
Who woke each hour from happy dreams of thee
To lay my smiling benison upon thy radiant soul?

DAY OF LIFE

—

TWAIN ONE

Day of Life
Rold White, author.
The Vine Press, Steyning; P.J. & A.E. Dobell, London. 1929.

Twain One
Rold White, author.
A. Merlyn Ward, cover illustration.
The Vine Press, Steyning; P.J. & A.E. Dobell, London. 1930.

It's easy to see why Victor Neuburg would become enamoured of the psychologist and poet Harold Dinely Jennings White. Each had an interest in liberation, of both body and spirit; each kicked against the cultural stasis of conservative England; each found his way in the '10s through acts of rebellion that would inform, and reverberate throughout, their lives. But while Neuburg was prone to flights of manic fancy and fantasy, White was profoundly steadfast in his beliefs and sure of both self and path. Vine Press published White's collected verse across two volumes, *Day of Life* in 1929 and *Twain One* in 1930, and the pair continued to communicate and work together for the rest of Neuburg's life.

H.D. Jennings White ('Rold' was Harold's youthful family nickname) was born in London in 1894; by the time of the First World War, he was unshakeable in his pacifism and was imprisoned as a conscientious objector. He used his detainment period well: already an educated man, White's time in labour camps focussed the mind and he began to connect the dots on a series of issues that would become his obsessions until the end of his long life. His work was as a psychologist – and a writer and educator in psychology – and as a philosopher. In the 1920s he was particularly interested in body acceptance, mental and physical health, and sexual freedom. A member of Edward Carpenter and Havelock Ellis's British Society for the Study of Sexual Psychology (BSSSP), White wrote on topics such as the positive aspects of nudism, homosexuality and sex before marriage.

One way in which White and Neuburg may have come to meet is through the Order of Woodcraft Chivalry, a pacifist (and, occasionally, pagan) response to the Boy Scouts. Both men wrote for the Order's newsletter, the *Pine Cone*, edited at one point by Sanctuary associate Dion Byngham. (Signs of the times: one of White's pieces for the *Pine Cone*, suggesting that, perhaps, masturbation wasn't the worst thing on earth, may have exacerbated a rift in the Order.) After the Vine Press years, White would work with Neuburg towards new ideas for criminal reform with the Association for the Scientific Treatment of Criminals, and to publish a series of White's philosophical writings in Neuburg's *Comment* magazine.

It's during the period in which he was detained as a conscientious objector that White wrote many of the poems included in *Day of Life* (1913–1921), which includes both works made before the war and pieces such as 'Poetic Reincarnation', written while working as a stone-breaker in a Carmarthen labour camp. *Twain One* collects more of these, but mostly poems written before or after the war, including his 'Jonathan' series made while working with Neuburg in the late-'20s, and poems with references to the landscapes around the Downs: White was at least an occasional, possibly regular, visitor to the Sanctuary and Vine Cottage.

After The Vine Press, White wouldn't publish another book of poetry, but his non-fiction bibliography went on to be sizable and varied. He published everything from *Goals of Life: For Students of Psychology and Ethics* to *Figure Skating Technique*. His writings as a philosopher were influential, and upon his death in 1977 *The Philosopher*, journal of the Philosophical Society of England, published a special issue dedicated to his life and work. Still, his book-length work on his philosophical system, *Eutrophia* – 'the full-blooded philosophy', serialised in Neuburg's *Comment* – remains as an analogue and unpublished manuscript. (Having married late, in his fifties, White's two children are still alive, providing a unique link to the Vine Press years for which we are very fortunate.)

Jean Overton Fuller incurred White's wrath when she published *The Magical Dilemma* by suggesting that 'Rold White' was a pseudonym of Neuburg's. The author hadn't published anything else under the name Rold White, his professional byline being either H.D. Jennings-White or simply Dr Jennings-White, and she mistook White's verse for his publisher's. A prickly exchange in the mid-1960s letters section of the

Times Literary Supplement followed publication of her biography, which resulted in bad blood between two people who could've been useful collaborators – White's archive from his Vine Press and *Comment* years ran deep. Instead, rather than include anything about White in later volumes, Fuller simply omitted the chapter in which she proposed White and 'Shirley Tarn' as Neuburg identities, leaving many – including the British Library catalogue – to continue listing the name as a pseudonym.

Dates and other notes on the Day of Life *poems are from White's archive, courtesy of his daughter, Margaret Jennings-White. Like the other books in this collection, the selections here have been left in the original Vine Press sequence, despite the dates of their creation. Poems from* Twain One *are mostly from the years immediately before and after the First World War.*

DAY OF LIFE

PROLOGUE: BIRTHDAY

To-day reminds us of our dim beginnings,
Foretells our distant ends, our destinies;
To-day we weigh our losses and our winnings,
Resolving discords into harmonies.

MORNING'S BIRTH

All is dark and still. . . .
Look o'er the distant hill
    A tinge of grey. . . .

Awake! Awake! Night's veil's withdrawn.
All hail! All hail, O Rosy Dawn!
        Oh haste Thy way!
        The East's aflame:
        All things proclaim
        " 'Tis Day!   'Tis Day!!"

MIST-DAWN

Cold and dank, the morning mist
Floats on the scumblown lake.

Cold and dank, the breath of night
Hangs on the pale dawn air.

Ghostly pallid, wraiths of grey
Hover and rift and rend.

Shreds of raiment, fairy-worn,
Gossamer phantoms whirl.

Cold and still, the thick moist air
Breathes o'er the water's sleep.

Pale dull-lustred crystal drops
Cling to the leaves and stones.

Glimmers here, peepholes there,
Slowly the mist-veil moves.

Glimpse of reeds and rushes slim
Bent by the water's edge.

Down the blind curtains droop
Over the dim-seen mere.

Dank and grey, a rifting glow
Looms from the heaving fog.

Grey grows slowly white, the dawn
Widens, brightens the light.

Still more swiftly lifts the haze:
Higher, lighter, brighter yet . . .
Dazzling, glorious . . . The Sun!

Written 1916.

NIGHT'S TEARS

May my desires not cry in vain,
Night; I crave thee, once again
Spread thy starry spangled net
With glittering constellations set,
Like a million jewelled eyes
Peeping through the curtained skies.
Breathe thy muted chords along,
Whose silence maketh evensong
One unuttered cosmic prayer
Issuing from everywhere.
Rising like rich frankincense
Thine opulent perfumes dispense;
And spill thy tears; and weep thy dew:
And all the tired world renew.

*Written 1 August 1919; White had been released from imprisonment
in January of that year.*

THE GREAT UNKNOWN

Days of life go spinning on;
Our little lives too soon are gone:
All things wax awhile, then wane;
All things rise to fall again.
Buds too soon become full-blown;
So too soon man's soul is thrown,
Unknowing, to the Great Unknown.

As the starlight's glittering ray,
Fading out at dawn of day,
Dies; and yet that star is there,
Far away, we know not where:
So, when all man's life is flown,
His body rots beneath a stone,
His spirit knows the Great Unknown.

INSANITY

To seek with aching brow and tortured heart
A home, a sanctuary, a place apart,
    A quiet paradise, a wholesome change
    From the ugliness of harsh reality.

To lose oneself in peaceful pleasant dreams,
Where fleeting phantasy's sweet shadow seems
    To take on lovelier forms of living fact
    While banishing the old reality.

To lift oneself above all earthly strife,
Beyond all greeds and lusts of human life,
    Beyond those cruel worlds of other men,
    And there create one's own reality.

DYING DREAMS

Lone, weak, and faint, I linger on,
Though all I lived for's lost, and dead, and gone,
And only echos of the music once was mine
My memories of paradise enshrine
With ghostly beauty, with sweet-bitter themes
That freeze my very tears, with dim dreams
Of all I loved and lived long days ago,
When all was joy and life, a merry show
Of pageantry and pleasure all too brief …
But now the grey and godless years of grief
Turn my soul slowly to cold stone,
And leave me blind, and silent, and alone.

TOWARDS DEATH

Weary, the dying light
Yields to the weary night. . . .

Stricken with anguish
At their unfruitfulness,
All my hopes languish
In utter weariness,
Brimmed deep with bitterness.

Dead is the life in me:
Death my last fealty.
All now is gone from me;
Even my enemy.

Death, how I long for Thee!
Thou, at the weary end,
Art the most trusted friend
In life's brief tragedy.

*'Dying Dreams' (27 June 1916) and 'Towards Death' (18 March
1916) were written while preparing his case for a tribunal on his
conscientious objection. His arguments failed and he was arrested 25
June 1917.*

WASTE

Hear'st thou the moaning of the restless sea,
How the waves roll down tempestuously
        And dash away their lives upon the shore?

Hear'st thou the groaning of humanity,
How men strive in blind activity
        And waste away their lives and nothing more?

RENAISSANCE

Out of the ashes that lie there cold on the hearth I rise,
Out of the ashes that seemed to be dead desire
I rise like the ghost of a flame that once was fire.

Out of my lips so long, so long now closed and mute,
Out of my lips a voice sings sweet and clear
The songs of joy that you once so loved to hear.

Out of my heart, so crushed with woes, so bruised, so torn,
Out of my heart new Love outspreads her wings
And heals all pain with Hope's foreshadowings.

Written in March, 1920, as White's life was returning to some kind of balance.

THE PRAYER OF THE PRODIGAL POET

Though I am stricken as one full of age,
Though my strength flickers like a guttering candle,
And my energy smoulders like a dying fire;
Yet, there is still in me the love of beauty,
Still the power of creation.
God, give me back the Muse that once could thrill
My soul with inspiration's easy skill;
Grant that I still may love, still shape my will,
May still the claims of artistry fulfil.
Fan the glowing flames of my desire.
Breathe into my soul the Breath of Fire.
Blow the whirling tempests of the Air:
And the great Waters of the Void dispart.
Show me WHO THOU ART,
The Whence, the Whither, and the Where.
Though old and stricken down in years,
Beaten and broken, blind with tears,
Wrinkled and seamed with griefs and cares,
Shattered by defeats and dread despairs,
Yet within this shrunken breast

Glows dauntless Hope that still the best
Shall burst from the unseen realms of thought
And set this strengthless death at nought.
Victorious with resurrected might
Shine through me once again, Thou Light of Light!

*Written 3 May 1917, at Woodbrooke Quaker Study Centre, near
Birmingham, where White was arrested a month later.*

POETIC REINCARNATION

"What are words? What are poems?"
Thus the searching student questioned,
As he sat and deeply pondered
On the still elusive wonder
Hid in springs of Poesy ....
Then a watchful quiet spirit
Soothed his craving brow, and smiling
Sang this song: –
"He that with the pangs of daring
Suffers through his mental bearing
Offspring of his soul and essence
Imaged of his inmost presence,
He creates a passing token,
Not a truth that, once 'tis spoken,
Is for evermore unchanging,
But a symbol onward ranging
Through the thoughts of others seeing
These the children of his being."
Then the Spirit ceased from singing.
And the student slowly waking
Held the Muse's revelation: –
"'Not a truth that, once 'tis spoken,

Is for evermore unchanging.'
Nothing I can write or fashion
Will endure, but time must crumble
All my labour into dust.
Yet my work's not unavailing:
Now I write for others' seeing,
Others seeing, understanding
With a mightier sense than mine;
Understanding, recreating
With a body more divine.
And so onward, ever onward,
In successive temples dwelling
Passes on the Truth that through me
Once in endless journeying passed.
Ever dying, recreating;
Changeless in reincarnating:
So the Spirit passes ever,
Staying in one body never."

*Written 30 August, 1918, while breaking stones in a prison labour
camp in Llanwrda, Carmarthenshire, Wales.*

EPILOGUE:

DAY OF LIFE

Each life upon its fated way-faring
Endures the cycle of a day, sharing
Its innocence with morning,
Its terror with the trial of night,
Its glory with the dawning light.

TWAIN ONE

FOREWORD

The design by A. Merlyn Ward depicts two lovers partaking of Divine Love under the symbols of Wine and Light.

In the initial verse the poet maintains that his art has its sources not in mere dreams, but is forged from his experience of reality. He intends it to help his readers live and love more fully.

The flow of thought then begins with the adolescent dream of love, recognises its dangers, and awakens to love's real desires and delights. 'Creative Love' reveals the merging of pity into love. The poet then tells how the fire of love when first kindled burns passionately, but as it afterwards increases, comes to shine with serene endless light; how love and contentment follow under the renunciation of selfish pride and luxury; how the supreme moment of lovers' union is felt as eternal. In 'Jonathan' the poet describes the three characteristic experiences after physical union, 'Love and Life', 'Love and Eternity', 'Love and Death'. Finally in 'Equanimity' we attain the end of the experiences of human love.

The sequence of the verses in 'Love Divine' begins with a restatement of the theme which closes 'Love Human', an affirmation of universal love. This is immediately followed by its negation. We then have a synthesis of these two opposing views by an exposition of the religious introvert's characteristic philosophy: – "as a man thinketh in his heart, so is he".

The succeeding poems develop the theme of mystic introversion. 'Sacrifice' depicts the desire of the neophyte at the beginning of the journey for the Vision, which seems so far away that the self seems to have no affinity with it and only the death of the self can win the prize. In the next poem we are shown a glimpse of Initiation; and, to counteract the apparent finality of this experience, in 'Thee' the poet reminds us that Beauty Absolute is 'still veiled'. In 'The Immortal Queen' is a repetition of the idea in 'Sacrifice' but with a more esoteric phantasy. 'Bliss Within' tells the same story but without the masochistic colouring. 'Adoration' lifts the experience beyond personal erotism into the spirit of the religious community. 'Radiant Light' expands the theme from the personal to the impersonal. 'Souls Alight' holds the warning that the mystical experience is dangerous. In 'Heavenly Wine' the poet attempts to depict the mystic ecstasy from the inside. In the final verse is focussed the motif: – 'two becoming one'.

The artist, the religious, the lover, insofar as they seek what is not themselves, are parts seeking wholedom.

THE LOVE-DREAM

I mages emerge from magic seas of thought,
Roll, and break like waves unbidden and unsought
Upon the faery shores of phantasy, where roam
The beings born of rainbows, bubbles, froth and foam
Floated by the wind. She comes, my Venus-Star,
From some fair realm of Beauty borne afar,
From some sweet Paradise, some Heaven above,
She comes all radiant with the light of Love.

. . . . .

O Dream of dreams, I pray thee with me stay,
And staying steal my real sense away.
Leave only dreams, leave only this one dream,
That dreaming love may ever real seem.

LOVE-DANGER

L ove lay dreaming o'er a precipice
      In ease secure,
Heeding not that dangerous abyss
      Which gulfs the pure.

Did Love dream on, drawing in innocent Sleep
      Unconscious breath;
Then, slowly slipping, swiftly through the deep
      Dash down to Death?

Did Love fling dreams aside, turn round, and face
      Real folk with Will,
Wise Power, and Skill; then humbly grace
      The living still?

LOVE

I n those eyes of blue I long to dwell,
  As 'twere some fairy sea-born shell
Wherefrom a fragrance pure doth well,
Enchanting me with happy spell,
Too exquisite for me to tell;
          Draw near
        That I may peer
      Into those luring deeps.

And, when entranced by beauty's sight,
I, dazzled, stand 'tween walls of light
And feel thy radiance rainbow-bright
Enrich my being with love's great might,

On some divine ethereal height
        I seem
     To stand and dream –
   Yet not as one who sleeps.

For the stress of earthly care slips past,
As into vague oblivion's vast
Its wearying strife is downward cast,
And o'er my soul gleams peace at last
As heart to heart I hold you fast –
        Twain one.
     'Tis Heaven begun:
   Love through our spirits sweeps!

LOVE'S SERENITY

I love thee more than passionately,
   I love thee in serenity.
For ever we could loving be
All through all time's eternity.
When, my belovèd, first we met
The stage for passionate love was set,
And we the players kindled fire,
And blazed with loving's fierce desire,
And mixed and mingled flame with flame,
And breathed each other's holy name:
But now the flame has burnt so bright,
So radiantly infinite,
For ever in Eternal Light
We love as wife and husband might,
United in one ecstasy
        Perpetual,
And need nor earth nor space nor time

To prove our mutual constancy;
For this is all
The sweetest secret of sublime
Eternal Love's serenity –
Bliss to be at one with thee!

THE GOLD MOON

The gold moon rose. . . .
And as we watched it silently
Float over the waters of the blue sea,
Filling the boundless deeps of the dark night
With glowing pools of scintillating light,
A wonder held us both in still trance,
As twain we watched the magic waters dance
And mix and mingle, intertwining
Light with liquid light, and shining
Like a million meteors melting in one
Great radiance, . . . or as if the sun
Dissolving into floods of golden light
Lay molten on the bosom of the night,
Pregnant with universal energy
Swelling and falling ever restlessly . . . . .
All held us, bound us, made us be as one
With all the bars between us all undone:
And oh, then shone within your beauteous eyes
Reflected lights of love, like bright fireflies
Or a thousand souls in dazzling robes of light,
Winging their infinite eternal flight.
Soon as my encircling arm would hold
Your lovely form close to my own, the gold
Shone into silver and a flood of white
Light lit up your beauty . . . such a sight,

I ... Those lips lay pressed upon my own,
Sweet flesh on flesh and sweetly bone on bone:
We breathed as one, as one our pulses leapt;
We lived as one, and one desire swept
Our whole being into living ecstasy,
Too lovely for the loveliest arts of poesy.

Like liquid pools of molten light
Mingling in the magic night
We melted into one delight.
One the love and one the life
Beyond all taint of self or strife
Inspired us when I called you "Wife".

That moment lives, lives like the breath
God breathes into the things of death;
Lives like the pulsing endless range
Of Life's full Being, Life's interchange
Of life with life. We are still one
Until all life and death be done,
One endless unity, one man-and-wife,
Endlessly infinite one life-in-life.

EQUANIMITY

No theme or thought of love is longer strong
Enough to make my tempered soul express
Its essence in impetuous excess
Of fiercely passionate impulsiveness.
My quiet dreams no more to love belong;
No passion makes my prose o'erflow in song:
No beauty wins me from my destiny;
(Once for a love I'd strip and fight with Fate,

And burn, and only end in agony).
Desireless, now, I live; beyond all hate,
Untouch'd by love, unmoved, I contemplate
The usual sequence of necessity.

FROM LOVE DIVINE

FATI AMOR

L ive, Passionate Life, live, live in my being.
Let both my eyes burn bright with their seeing.
Let all my senses swoon with their feeling
The pleasure of living, life's essence revealing.
Let me drink to each dreg what Fate's cup may contain.
Let me sink in each sound like the earth-loving rain
Swift dies in the ground, or the sea, or the fire . . .
No matter what; 'tis my only desire,
Whatever kind God or blind Destiny brings,
To be one with, to die in, unite with all things.
Oh, burn me, or drown me, or grind me to dust,
I love Thee, O World, for love Thee I must.

NOW HAVE I LOOKED UNTO THE END

H elpless each soul's in fleshly prison pining,
Torn in between desire and desire;
One craving ever in another twining,
Binding the soul with hungering tongues of fire.

257

Ever does greed recoil in its own yearning:
    Ever does goal recede as goals are won.
There is no end to all this quenchless burning,
    No end, until the whole life's span be done;

No end to torture, while the soul aspiring
    Grows dizzier with satisfaction won;
No end, till all this lust at last expiring
    Falls into ashes when the life is done.

SACRIFICE

O Radiant Vision, all things of earth transcending,
From spheres of perfect Lovelyness descending,
What would I not accomplish in Thy Cause,
Keep what commandments, break what sacred laws!
But only one thing is required of me: –
To break myself and keep what is not me.
One thing alone dost Thou require of me: –
To die, that I may be reborn as Thee.

PHANTASY
AND
OTHER POEMS

THE HERMES BOOKS:

NUMBER TWO

Phantasy and Other Poems
The Hermes Books: Number Two
Ethel Archer, author.
The Vine Press, London & Steyning. 1930.

The esoteric modernism of Vine Press found no better textual expression than in the project's final outing, Ethel Archer's book of poems past and present, *Phantasy*. Full-circle, in some ways, from Neuburg's own *Triumph of Pan*, the titular sequence in Archer's small book is ripe with dark forests and 'Simian dwarves'; pastoral sheep-bells, the Formless and the Misbegotten. Archer's dedications describe her influences from the London literary and esoteric worlds she moved through with native ease: fantasy writer and Yeats associate Lord Dunsany; *Occult Review* editor Harry J. Strutton; London bookdealer Arthur Probsthain, specialising in 'African and Oriental' works; novelist and wine merchant Ernest Oldmeadow. Florid and fantastical, *Phantasy* dresses in occult rags, but at its heart resonates mostly with a love of dreaming – of disappearing into a masque of life when the real thing seems, at best, unlikely.

Ethel Florence Edith Archer was born in Slaugham, Sussex, in 1885. As a young woman she fell in love with a poor artist of French origin named Eugene Wieland and, in around 1908, they were married. The couple was absurdly in love – the passion of their early marriage was voyeuristically narrated by the American writer Elizabeth Robins Pennell, who watched them from her window and recounted their life, as seen this way, in *The Century Illustrated* magazine. Soon after they wed, the pair fell in with Aleister Crowley, with Wieland becoming his 'personal secretary'. They attended events in Crowley's home, and soon were part of his inner circle, with both Eugene and Ethel working on *The Equinox* magazine – which also published her first book, *The Whirlpool*, soon after doing the same with *The Triumph of Pan*. Neuburg became a close friend – in fact, her descriptions of Vickybird to Jean Overton Fuller (as Puck-like), and her quoting of the publisher in *Phantasy*, point to an essence of Neuburg in *Phantasy* itself.

In 1915, Eugene J. Wieland was killed on the first day of the battle of Loos. His bravery is the stuff of film: at Givenchy, he ran, alone, across the field of battle to help rescue a unit stranded when their trench collapsed, literally tearing his shirt into bandages. While injured at Loos, his leg shattered in no-man's-land, awaiting stretcher-bearers, he scribbled notes on enemy placements for his commanding officer. His death was to define Ethel for the rest of her life: she never remarried, and she would die nearly 50 years later at the same address she had shared with Eugene, still legally bearing his name. And yet, as Ethel Archer, she would continue to have a rich life as a writer and activist. In the '30s she fictionalised her life with Wieland, their time with Crowley and Neuburg, and the solace she sought in Bohemianism, in her novel *The Hieroglyph*. She wrote reviews and articles for the *Occult Review* and other publications for years to come. Later in the '30s she became active in anti-fascist politics, and worked with Sylvia Pankhurst in the campaign to aid Ethiopia against Italian aggression.

As the second of the Hermes Books, following Shirley Tarn's *Seven Years* (notably, the amount of time she and Wieland were married), *Phantasy* is another no-frills collection without the beloved Vine Press illustrations and containing disparate work written over a long period of time – some of the additional poems date to circa. 1900, and the long piece, *Phantasy* itself, was begun before the war, but only finished for this publication (and, it would seem, with Neuburg's and Lord Dunsany's final push). Yet, in its association with Neuburg's London life, *Phantasy* brings an appropriate closure to the Vine Press odyssey.

By 1931, Neuburg was back to living primarily in London, although he visited Vine Cottage regularly for some time: he was still bringing guests for literary weekends in the summer of 1933. His marriage had ended, though he and Kathleen never divorced, and he was shacked-up with Runia MacLeod at her Primrose Hill artist's studio. The Vine Press – its typeface, at least – was given to the West brothers for their printing business and shop, which lasted in Steyning High Street until the 1990s. (The whereabouts of that unique type are, today, unknown: it was possibly given to the Amberley Working Museum in the 1980s, but regardless, has disappeared.)

Hayter Preston would soon give his old friend a brief but famous tenure running Poet's Corner for *Sunday Referee*, and Victor Neuburg would ultimately be without a Press to call his own, and yet – as he had wanted to be – 'back in the swim' of life in the literary capital.

The selections that follow include the entirety of the 'Phantasy' sequence as well as selected other pieces from the book.

PHANTASY

ARGUMENT

The writer falls asleep in a wood at dusk.

During his sleep a thunderstorm comes on, and his dream is peopled with the beings of ancient phantasy.

The really active spirits are Pan and his followers, and these all unconsciously influence the other phantoms of his dream. Thus, when the Pan-pipes are playing merrily, the people of the Court are happy; when the strains are softer and slower, they become sad.

Throughout the dream the fairy music continues, taking him from the Court of Phantasy, where the Knight "Romance" dallies with his faire ladye, back to the woodland, where he sees two lovers who have strayed away from the rest, and in their wanderings have caught Pan sleeping. The god vanishes, but the transitory glimpse has taught them to solve his mystery by solving the mystery of themselves.

This realised, they are returning happily homewards when they come in contact with the other people of the Court.

These, (each separately aware of his own guilt), are talking scandal, to the accompaniment of the envious elves and the swaying hemlock, until the whole wood has become darkened with their malice. Thus, temporarily, the music stops.

But the happy lovers, immortalised through their grand discovery; having disarmed hate and suspicion, a strange and wondrous silence ensues. This is broken by the youngest poet of the Court of Phantasy, "One who from the crowd has wandered, thinking thoughts of Love and Sorrow". In a two-fold Hymn to Luna he voices the thoughts and aspirations of the enlightened crowd. The Hymn dies away in an amplified echo from the distance, this echo enlarging the theme.

The sleeper is awakened at Dawn by the tinkling of a distant sheep-bell.

INTRODUCTION

I WANDERED out at dew-fall,
And alone
Heard the soft-soughing of the dusk-clad pines
Sink to a shuddering whisper;
Till anon,
The blue-cowled lightning struck the quivering shade,
Waking the thousand images of Eld
That slumbered.
Weirdly-wise
Troop they un-numbered from the listening dells
Of snake-infested silence.
Charmëd bells
Tinkle a wondrous music as they go,
Like to the frozen melody that wells
From the thin-reeded river.
Joyous elves
Dance with abandon in the cumbrous shade
Of monstrous gnomes,
(Whose lurching gait they mimic),
Whilst there swells
A changeless, changing rhythm,
Wherein dwells,
Recurring ever, (as the faëry spells
Got of long ages),
One frail glass-like note.

Across the forest carpeted with pine,
Within the shadow of the mighty elms,
The strange sound drew me, till,
Crouched in the hollow of an old, old oak,

Found I an agëd Pan,
Playing upon a pipe of river reeds.
His long beard blew
Over his fingers, as their magic drew
The old enchantment; till the dryads ran,
Laughing, to meet him; and the elfin crew,
Hid i' the branches, mischief great did plan.

The lucid mantle of the large-eyed moon
Lay in its golden glamour over all;
How daintily they let the fir-cones fall!
Laughing to see them roll, as children do;
And all the while the magic murmur grew,
For Pan was merry on this night of June!

Into the forest stepping silently
Came haughty ladies from a Court long dead,
Talking in dulcet tones to lords who bled
Years since in battle, duel, or some fray
Wrought by the amorous god. How blithely gay
Seems now their converse, tripping jauntily,
Now falling sadly, as the music strays
In softer mood, even as the player plays.

For Pan they see not, though the fairy glade
Throng with his followers. Their stiff brocade
Rustles no louder though some winsome sprite
Lurk in the folds, who laughing tries to bite
The coral ear wherefrom some jewel weighs,
Stirring to envy all his heart's delight.

They know not whence that sylvan music springs,
Touching the triple chord of ecstasy;
Nor yet the passing memory it brings,
Fraught with the soul of all the woodland things
Born in the night.

They only feel the subtle sorccery
Of summer madness, when the tangled hair
Of some bright nymph has caught them unaware,
Adding her kisses to the dimpled breeze,
Laughing to Pan deep hid within the trees,
Still playing, playing, to the summer air.

O magic night of Love and Secrecy!
Soft stars are trailing through the amber dusk,
A nameless mystery surrounds the husk
Of life new-breaking. O the sapphire sea
Pearled with its foam of stars!
The crystal key
Whereof who holds, knows not Life's anarchy.

I watched from out the shadows warily,
And marked the passing pageant as it flowed
In rhythmic wonder down the winding road:
The darkened forest – monstrous effigy
Of Simian dwarfs with twisted limbs, that flee
The moving shadows – till the darkness grows
One phosphor flame, more frail than elfin snows
Wherein I founder. Swiftly, silently,
The dream clouds o'er me, as a limpid sea
Of gloom-voiced laughter, echoing eerily,
Fades in the distance. Endlessly it flows,
This strange procession, as some spiral goes,
And I must follow, whither no man knows.

PHANTASY

S O, to that ancient Court, where Phantasy
Sleeps in the moonlight, and the knight Romance,
Visored and plumed, and armed for errantry,
Haunts yet the dewy sward. His charger, gay
With silken trappings, champs impatiently,
Pawing the lawn, the while for one last glance
His master lingers. Can his lady say
When next their meeting? Whether far away
In some fell foreign land, or where the may
Powders the hedge rows? But the silence knows;
And, gravely gay, she kisses tenderly
The wild wet rose; then throws it to him. They,
The Sisters Three, shall surely guard him! Nay,
Must guard him. So, they part. And still the strain
Of fairy music echoes. As a flute
Silverly-sweet, the fountain tumbles. Mute,
The shadows hasten to the marble brim,
Melting in mist, and merge themselves; or float
Like argent lilies on a mystic moat
Guarded by moon-beams. For the fairies' whim
Is ever to seem beautiful, and feign
Beauties they know not of, so they may chain
All beauty to them. So I dreamed.
                     Again,
Lost in the aureole of the moon's bright hair,
I saw two Lovers turning. Deathly fair
Were their pale features, for a glad despair
Born of too strange a knowledge kept them there,
Lured by the forest, that for days had known
Their sweet communion. Silently, alone,
Through the vast wood they wandered, and at morn
Had found the Wood-God sleeping. Round him, torn,
Lay scattered leaves and flower garlands. Torn

Was his goatish beard, and likewise torn
The floating garment of some wood-nymph – (born
Say of what midnight struggle!) – for her hair,
Fragrant as dawn and light as gossamer,
Lay yet within his grasp. The astonished pair
Scarce caught the vision ere the monster woke,
Saw them, and vanished. And before them, there,
Grey in the sunshine, was an agëd oak,
Crabbed, gnarled, and rotten, – the decaying stem
Covered with mossy growths; and binding them,
Just where one limb protruded, hung a haze,
Sliv'ry and fine – a silken spider's maze.
So still they wander seeking him: and Night
Follows the Day, and from her azure steep
The Moon looks down and loves them; and soft Sleep
Weaves them her poppied mantle, and they creep
Deep down within the folds, and oft-times weep
For very happiness of dear delight.

Once more a vision; and the fountain-court
Is filled with lords and ladies, and the sport
Of whispering elves and mannikins is fraught
With dire intention. Sinister with Thought
The pine trees shiver. In the listening gloom
Pale ghostly moths flit phantom-wise, and loom
Silent as ashen Fate, whose eyes' still doom
Sees in the mouldering Past the Future's tomb,
Nor waits for any man. The gold-orbed Moon,
(A luminous void within the indigo),
Droops down behind the trees, whose gaunt arms trace
Sad violet sigils that the winds embrace,
Scattering the fallen leaves. About the place
The strange sounds linger, imminent and slow,
Like vast dim echoes of the worlds' great race,
Rung from the chains of inter-stellar space
Circling immensity. Then silence, so

My heart may hear its beating, and I know
Not what of fell interpretation lends
Itself to my soul's secrecy, and blends
All loftier magic with that still small rune.
But I am silent, and I mark the tune
Of the silver showers of the fountain, and the swoon
Of the great silver stars, as each one bends
In lofty adoration, and descends
To bathe in her own beauty; and the tears
Of all the fettered phantasms of years
Seem subtly intermingling in the whirl
Of this strange Universe, whose voices curl
In blind 'fantastic nautch'*; till Darkness furl
The flags of the wind, and down the ravine hurl
The tattered hosts. So, to oblivion.
Then, 'mid the shadow of the dreaming yews,
Strange Night-Shapes gather; and pale ghastly dews
Drip from their ice-cold fingers, to infuse
With deadly malison the woodland round.
The deadly night-shade steals from out the ground,
And the lank hemlock casts its fatal flower
About the ivied slopes, where seems to cower
The ancient memory of evil things,
The Formless and the Misbegotten. Wings,
Bat-like and envious, beat the lowering air
In ever lessening circles, (as Despair,
That shapes but its own orbit, yet must dare
Endlessly to escape, the while aware
Of its own impotence.) An awful glare
Lights up the woodland, as each guilty pair
Halts in mid-darkness, seeming to declare
The other's thought: then, feigning ignorance,

* This phrase is borrowed from V.B.N.

Each keeps the narrow circle, moving on
At the same pace: the one ignoble fear
Goading all minds in secret, that they share
Their neighbour's haunt. O hateful variance
Of Truth with Custom, Reason with Romance!
Courage, as virtue, reaps her fair reward;
Virtue, as cowardice, is rightly scored:
And ye are cowards all, yet each must taunt
With trivial spite the other, so to vaunt
Better his perfect self. And so they walk,
Whispering scandal, to the poinsoned talk
Of envious elves, whose council is to balk
All human happiness. And yet more near
The tall shapes gather, and a new-born fear,
Creeping by stealth amid the listening trees,
Stirs in their topmost branches. Ill at ease
The faint leaves rustle, as they strive to share
The winds' low secret.

      As a bird of sable plumage
      Rising from a stormy ocean,
      Sweeps the Night across the hill-tops;
      Ruffled are his shining feathers,
      All his wings are dashed with water,
      Drops which falling dull earth's torches,
      Drown the stars in all their glory:
      Then the pale-faced moon in terror
      Draws a veil across her features,
      Bows her weeping head in silence,
      Praying for the stars, her children.
      But the Night recks naught of sorrow,
      Scornfully he rushes onward,
      Shakes anew his gloomy pinions,
      While his yellow eyes dart lightning.
      From his cave beneath the mountains
      Warily the Sun-God watches,

Shakes his crested head in anger,
Fixes flaming eyes upon him;
Yet the Night draws on undaunted.

In the distance, through the darkness,
From without the whirling tempest,
Comes the sound of happy voices,
Sweetest sounds of sweeter converse,
Love confessed to Love's Confessor:
And the steadfast pair returning,
Touched not by the storm around them,
Tell a tale of wondrous beauty,
Tell a tale whereon they marvel,
While the light of a great gladness
Rests upon their happy faces:
Thus they sing, the youthful Lovers,
Love brought safely through the Darkness.

"Far within the distant woodland
We have found the great Pan sleeping,
And in vanishing he left us
For the greater God Who made him;
And a knowledge all transcendent
Lighteth up the world around us:
We have found the inmost meaning
Of the sun-beam and the dew-drop,
Of the hush of winds at evening,
And the pleasant summer pastures;
Love alone is of God's nature,
Wherefore true love must be God-like,
And the love of meanest creature
Adds but to His praise and glory;
Each within the other, finding
Image of himself transcended,
Knows at last the greater union
Wherein all things must be blended;

Finds his God, and God instructs him:
Love alone is key to all things,
Earthly love, the pale reflection
Of that greater Love whose glory
Fills the earth and floods the Heaven;
Of that greater Love whose glory
Seen alone on earth would blind us;
Yet we seek it; ever turning
Strife to Life, and darkness spurning."

Then upon that sombre woodland,
Full of sounds of whispered malice,
Falls a strange and wondrous silence,
Sweeter than the sound of harp-strings,
Than the distant sound of harp-strings,
Than the memory of music
When the heart for love is silent.
And one, youngest of the poets,
Foundling of the Court of Fancy,
One who from the crowd has wandered,
Thinking thoughts of love and sorrow,
Lifts his child-clear voice to Heaven,
With his child-pure brow adoring,
Making songs of fair entreaty
To the white-veiled Queen of Heaven,
And the whole wide wood is silent.

TO THE MOON SPIRIT

"O BRIGHT and glorious Spirit, born of air,
Thou angel-guardian of the silver moon,
That read'st with solemn awe her mysteries,
And, like the Jewish patriarch of old
Stand'st on the Threshold dread with veilëd face,
Fearful to show mankind its auguries:
Remove the cloud that hides thee from my gaze!
Reveal thyself in beauty, heavenly rare,
And give me insight to the mystery
Surrounds thy radiant being, and the key
That access gives to the bright spirit world
Whose god-like speech strikes not dull mortal ears.
Say what thy mind doth pass, as, through the night,
The windswept clouds are tossed about thy brow,
The pale gold orb o'er Earth and Heaven doth shine,
And all around is peace most loneliest?
What fearful secret lock'st thou in thy breast?
What vague unholy terrors dost thou see,
Whilst looking down with calm benignant eye
Upon the still and sleeping earth beneath?
Say, ever does mankind in wildest thought
Think thou art witnessëd of all their deeds,
Or that thy bright and dazzling face is dulled
By looking on their crime and misery?
To man thou speak'st not, but perchance to God
Thou tell'st a mingled tale of joy and woe,
Reflected in thine own all-glorious face
To mortal eyes which seems so passionless.
If this be so, thou need'st must know the fate
Impending on our one and every deed;
And, as thou roamest through the worlds of space,
With prophet eye foresee our destiny.
But only, glorious Spirit, give to me

The power to sing thy praises far and wide,
An I renounce all vain ambition else,
And, as thy chaunter, I am satisfied.

"O Luna, who, when Night's black shadow, creeping
Like some dark vision, doth the world enfold,
Dost shed thy silver light whilst stars are peeping,
And earth's round orb onward in space hath roll'd;
O Luna, beautiful, pure, fair, and stately,
What poet hath not of thy praises sung?
What wanderer lone hath not been gladdened greatly
When thou in Heaven hast like a lantern hung,
And pointed out to him his homeward way,
And where-through all the shades of Night it lay?

"O Luna fair, what hast thou not beholden
From thy high throne in Heaven's cloudless space,
When thou hast watched until the sunlight golden
Hath filled each babbling brook and shady place?
What bloody battlefields hast thou looked down on?
What paramours have met beneath thy light?
What naïads of the wood with myrtle crown on
Have danced and sported all the livelong Night?
Till Dawn hath come, and they have fled way,
For nymoh and naïad ne'er are seen by day.

"O Queen of Heaven! Look down on every nation,
And let thy gentle peace steal in our heart;
Teach the whole world with all the blest creation
To know, and each to do, his destined part.
Set us thy pure example, that, thee seeing,
Upward to higher regions may we soar,
Beyond the thought and sight of mortal being,
Where mortal man hath never trod before;
Teach us to gladly know the one true Will,
And whilst on earth we live, pursue it still."

(*Distant echo.*)

"The one true Will, to which all wills be turning;
The Vision of the Universe, set free
From Adam's curse. Pan and his nymphs returning
Back to the woods; and fairest minstrelsy
Limning the earth."

(*Fainter still,*
but very clear.)

"All things a manner of our mode of seeing,
And Love the quest and answer to our Being."

EPILOGUE

SOFT as the brooding Dove whose love-swift wings
From the high heaven sped downward, when of old
She saw, and seeing, loved the King of Kings,
Shadowing His sacred head from the fierce heat;
So dies the song. And swift the morning's gold
Spreads slowly. On the hills the dew is sweet.

The silent voices of the Dawn
Are waking round me, Life is still;
And Death in transport seems as Life,
The Higher Servant of the Will:
I know not if I die or live,
Or if I move or cease to be,
Save only that within my heart
Lies Love's untrammelled ecstasy.

WAX:

A DRAMA OF EVOLUTION

Wax: A Drama of Evolution
Runia MacLeod, author.
The Vine Press Ltd., London. 1947.

Victor B. Neuburg died in 1940, a year after his mother and in the same place: a home in the Swiss Cottage area of London owned by his partner, the enigmatic feminist writer and critic Runia MacLeod. The two were together for the last ten years of Neuburg's life, probably since at least 1929 – when MacLeod's surrealistic, dystopian-feminist play *Wax* was originally written. *Wax* wasn't published until its author undertook a small run of 250 copies (which may have actually only been 200) in 1947, making it the first of two books under the Vine Press name after Neuburg's death. But the people and work of The Vine Press had an obvious influence on MacLeod's writing, and vice-versa, and the play was almost certainly discussed initially as a Vine Press publication. For these reasons, it seems only correct to include it as a posthumous addition to the original Vine Press canon.

Runia MacLeod* is a fascinating character – as much an expression of the first half of Britain's 20th century as she was a thorn in its side. The woman who came to be called Runia MacLeod was born Ethel Winifred Elizabeth Simpson in 1879 in imperial India, where her father was deputy commissioner of the Madras police. She was shipped home to Britain for

---

* It's worth adding a note on Runia's name. 'Runia MacLeod' is the name which this woman chose for her Vine Press publication, and is therefore the one we will use, but she went by many others: Ethel or Winifred Simpson became Carter and then Tharp; for a while in the 1920s and '30s she was Runia Tharp, and then Sheila MacLeod and Runia MacLeod, both of which, as well as Tharp, she used until her death in 1970, at 90 years old. (Her grandchildren knew her as 'Granny MacLeod'.) There seems to be no direct line to the names 'Sheila', 'Runia' or 'MacLeod' other than her interests and extremely powerful will.

schooling, finding herself alone at a young age in a 'homeland' that was utterly foreign to her. From the dawn of the 20th century, she was fiercely independent, a passionate suffragette and a dedicated modernist when it came to the arts, literature, and, most rebelliously, love. At one point her first husband, the painter and art educator Leslie Augustus Bellin-Carter, and her second husband, painter Charles Julian Theodore Tharp, lived with her together in Bellin-Carter's home just a few miles from the site of the Sanctuary in Sussex.

At some point in the 1920s, she met Victor B. Neuburg. Each was married with children, but both marriages were, by that point, agreements more than relationships, and it wasn't long before Neuburg was splitting his time between Vine Cottage and the Primrose Hill studio MacLeod shared with her husband and sons. Soon, together, they left for St John's Wood, and it was there that things began to – finally, and oh-so-briefly – come together for each of them. MacLeod was instrumental in Neuburg's work at Poet's Corner, and like him she was an early champion of Dylan Thomas, despite the Welshman's private disparaging of each of them. Their home became a centre for London's literary, artistic and political edges, a social status that became professional when MacLeod helped found *Comment* weekly magazine. (*Comment* rose from the ashes of Neuburg's work editing poetry for *Sunday Referee*, a position which had spawned a tight-knit social circle wanting for a home after he was suddenly terminated.)

From late-1935 until mid-1937, *Comment* operated from MacLeod's home: she and Vickybird edited it; they each wrote multiple columns; they raised its funds, and then redistributed most of those. The paper itself was assembled by their circle of friends and admirers in the Boundary Road home, and printed by local communist printers – who withdrew their support when Neuburg informed them that he supported them, but would never himself be a communist, anarchism having completely entranced his political heart. *Comment* almost certainly never broke even, and acts as a final, beautiful-loser masterpiece for Neuburg and MacLeod.

In 1937, Victor's health failing and their printers balking, Runia MacLeod shut down *Comment* and turned her attentions to caring for him and his similarly ailing mother: between 1939 and 1940, the Neuburgs, mother and son, died.

MacLeod's sole published fictional work, *Wax*, was originally conceived as a film screenplay in 1929, and she tried her damnedest to get that film made. But it's hard to see how commercial studios of the time might respond positively to its surrealistic feminist vision. *Wax* appears to be influenced by Japanese Noh theatre and Medieval mystery plays; by H.D. Jennings White and Edward Carpenter and Emmeline Pankhurst. And its autobiographical elements – its composites are thinly veiled – make it deeply personal. In 1931, Hayter Preston passed a revised-for-stage version along to the Irish playwright Sean O'Casey, who liked it enough to give Runia a 'kindly message of encouragement', but apparently not enough to do much else.

So in 1947, reeling from loss, still in Boundary Road with her youngest son and his wife, Runia revived The Vine Press at least in name and published her small run of *Wax*. Her friend, the surrealist artist and renowned psychotherapist Grace Pailthorpe, wrote of the play, 'Are we moderns at the threshold of a higher evolution, or are we going down into decay like the nations of the past? *Wax*, in answering this question, through the inescapable logic of its human drama, must be read and seen by all who would have a keener insight into the future of the human race.' But there was little else to be said of it. Reviews or even mentions were few and far between, and it has never been performed.

FROM *WAX*, ACT I:

... RUTH remains silently smoking and gazing at EMILY
VINER. *She is not aware for some seconds that charming
little* GRADY O'HARA *has entered and is hesitating at
her table with an armful of parcels).*

RUTH: Oh, Grady, what joyous chance brought you to-day?

GRADY Pat's been so lucky with his fruit and bees that he insisted
O'HARA: on my celebrating at the sales. And I've got some *gorgeous*
bargains. (*Nods her head towards the parcels scattered on
the floor.*) What d'you think, Ruth, one of the new ...

RUTH: (*gently as to a child and checking grady's gesture to open a
parcel*) I'd love to see them all sometime, Grady dear. But
tell me now (*nods towards* EMILY VINER), do you
recognise her?

GRADY: Indeed, I do not. And yet I do. . . . Wait a minute now,
where have I seen her? It can't be ... Emily Viner?

RUTH: You know why, of course?

GRADY: It's through, is it? Well, she waited till she was sure, poor
soul. I admire her for that.

RUTH: (*gloomily*) Can one ever be sure? I mean, of hopelessness?

GRADY: (*looking at her friend with concerned affectionate eyes*) It's a
holiday you'll be wanting, Ruth. Listen to me, now. You
come back home with me to-morrow for a week. Bring
a pile of your precious old books with you. Pat's always
saying it's Ruth Trevor he'd rather have than any, because
she takes so little attending to.

RUTH: (*smiling*) My dear, there's nothing I'd like better, but we are in the midst of a book flood. I'm broadcasting and have two lectures this week. One out of town this very afternoon.

GRADY: But Ruth, it's lecturing that surely kills you.

RUTH: (*steering past this remark*) So you see it's impossible. But thank you, Grady, and if I can possibly squeeze in a week before the children's holidays, may I come then? How *are* Pat and his famous bees?
(**EMILY VINER** *and* **LORIMER MUIRHEAD** *have come up to* **RUTH'S** *table and the four women greet each other in the informal club way, as the newcomers draw up two smaller chairs*).

LORIMER   Yes, how are the famous bees? Mr O'Hara's a bit of an
MUIRHEAD: expert, isn't he?

GRADY: Pat says they're the most civilised creatures on this earth. The more he knows of them, the more advanced he thinks them. He says they're super-civilised.

EMILY
VINER: Even beyond man?

GRADY: (*sparkling with delight at holding the group of women with her husband's views, which she proceeds to rattle off categorically*) Man has to have more science before he can understand their methods. They practise birth-control and adjust sex numbers to national needs; they're marvellous geometricians, and they've discovered a wireless system of attaining a *perfect simultaneous working of the communal will* that so far we can only guess at.

RUTH: (*rather playfully completing the mechanical eulogy*) And sure there's nothing they don't know about glands?

LORIMER
MUIRHEAD: Glands! Why glands?

RUTH: Oh, they're the newest Great-Solution-of-All-Problems, aren't they?

EMILY
VINER: Including that of the effeminate youths of to-day?

LORIMER (*contemptuously*) And possibly our return to long
MUIRHEAD: skirts? I wonder how that attempt will really end. I mean that masculine bid through fashion to involve our energies once more with hair and skirts.

EMILY (*sardonically*) Evidently some handicap has been
VINER: found necessary.

RUTH: Wigs and draped limbs really died with the last of feudalism. It seems to me that this reversion is only a temporary defiance on our part—a "we'll-damn-well-do-as-we-please" gesture. (*Dully*) In the end we'll be drawn into the rigid economic necessity of uniform, like men.

LORIMER (*brightly*) I hear they've evolved the perfect feminine
MUIRHEAD: trouser. Would you wear it?

EMILY
VINER: { I'd like to.
        (*together*)
RUTH: { It would be horribly convenient.

GRADY I saw the sweetest little suits on the films—skirt with
O'HARA: braces, silk shirt and tailor-made coat. One felt at once "That's just what I've been needing without knowing it."

EMILY
VINER: I believe this officious fashion influence will bring about the very thing it's struggling against—and trousers will arrive with a bound.

GRADY
O'HARA: (*trying to renew her delicious experience of an attentive audience*) Pat says that at some time or other before history, bees must have had a sex war and so evolved the neuter.

EMILY
VINER
and RUTH: (*startled and fascinated. A mutual glance of understanding passes between them. From this moment to the end of the act the conversation is detached and impersonal*) The neuter! Of course! Freedom from sex!

RUTH: (*continuing*) As a result of scientific experiment with glands?

LORIMER
MUIRHEAD: (*in a dry legal manner without any emotional or humorous suggestion*) Experiment's in the air——

GRADY
O'HARA: Especially in sex, my dears, there seems no decent limit.

RUTH: Should there be a limit to experience? It provides the answer—and one's own experience for choice—every time.

EMILY
VINER: I should like to see some experiment in sex-control myself.

LORIMER
MUIRHEAD: Quite a number of women with a real antipathy to marriage, or any union that includes a common daily life with a man, desire a personal experience of motherhood.

GRADY
O'HARA: Poor souls, and what do they do about it?

these war-destroyers and their aftermath of drifters are to
go on in everlasting sequence. . . .

LORIMER   *(looks at her with the superior regard of a professional,*
MUIRHEAD: *good-naturedly watching the forensic preserves being cropped*
by an amateur, facetiously aside to **GRADY**) We say
"**NO WAR**" to men, and they retort "to whore or not to
whore", eh?
(**GRADY'S** *face turns from one to the other with a*
shrinking, horrified, yet fascinated gaze.)

EMILY   *(Ends on a note of menace that releases a terrific sense of*
VINER: *injury)* . . . then . . . **THEN** . . . **SEX WAR LIKE THE**
BEES!

CURTAIN
(End of Act I)

CHAPBOOKS:

A BIBLIOGRAPHY OF REFERENCES TO ENGLISH AND AMERICAN CHAPBOOK LITERATURE OF THE EIGHTEENTH AND NINETEENTH CENTURIES

Chapbooks: a bibliography of references to English and American Chapbook Literature of the eighteenth and nineteenth centuries
Victor E. Neuburg, author.
The Vine Press, London. 1964.

In 1964, a final instalment in the Vine Press catalogue was issued. Victor E. Neuburg ('Toby'), Vickybird and Kathleen's son, published his *Chapbooks: a bibliography of references to English and American Chapbook Literature of the eighteenth and nineteenth centuries* – a slight, zine-like production consolidating its author's obsession with, and deep historical knowledge of, early street literature. Produced in small numbers and sold only through Toby's house and the Southwood Bookshop (more recently known as Ripping Yarns bookshop) in Highgate, London.

Chapbooks is, first and foremost, a bibliography: besides its brief introduction, it is not particularly compelling reading for most of us, although there is a poetry to its listings – entire histories, lifetimes, spent within the pages mentioned, in the way that connoisseurs of sport can reimagine long-ago actions through stats and tables. But it is also, in an unstated way, a dedication to Toby's father and his life's work of reinvigorating the street ballad and its anonymous balladeer; the lovingly printed page and its decadent creator.

'I have taken the term "chapbook" to include not only the little books which were hawked throughout this country and the American Colonies during the Eighteenth Century, but also their survivals and successors in the Nineteenth,' writes Toby in the preface. 'This includes street ballads, execution sheets, "last dying speeches" and other fugitive papers which achieved extraordinarily wide circulations before the days of the cheap press...'

What could please the ostrobogulous mind of Victor B. Neuburg more than his son taking, as his subject matter, 'fugitive papers' of mad 18th-century poem-hawkers?

Victor E's book is a true Vine Press publication – even using the signature, 1920s Steyning tree wood-cut as its title-page insignia. And it is a fitting tribute to that project. In the book's introduction, Victor E. Neuburg may well be speaking of his father when he describes the work of the 'chapman' in the 18ᵗʰ and 19ᵗʰ centuries:

'An important part of his stock-in-trade had become a budget of small books, whose varied subject matter included devils, angels, scoundrels, heroes, love, hate, fairy tales, religion, fables, shipwreck, executions, prophecies and fortune telling. Illustrated with woodcuts, they cost usually one penny each.'

Chapbooks is a bibliography, and a love-letter; it is Toby's opportunity to TAP (Take A Pew) and give thanks to his father for the devils and angels, scoundrels and heroes, love and hate and prophecy.

AFTERWORD

BY MARGARET JENNINGS-WHITE

When Justin contacted me hoping that I was indeed the 'closest living link to the Vine Press', as the eldest daughter of Press author Rold White, I was intrigued. I knew I had poetry books, letters and pictures – but where? Boxes labelled 'Keep now, sort later' are fundamental to a family of hoarders! Little did I know that that maxim would unearth so much of interest, some of which is now captured in *Obsolete Spells*. My own memories were rekindled – of growing up in Northwest London and my college days in Sussex – and were connected to the snippets of my Father's life that he had cared to share.

The jigsaw of his 'being' had many pieces that I couldn't quite fit into the bigger picture of his life, from 1894 to 1977. He was a private man who needed peace and quiet. I knew there were books of poetry, but sadly, I never asked him directly about their origins or how they came to be published by The Vine Press. I remembered frank exchanges with regard to authorship of his poems and knew that I had that correspondence somewhere. But trawling through his somewhat unorganised archives of diaries, letters, papers, lecture notes, publications, and many poems, I unearthed so much more.

This was my Father.

I discovered that the majority of his poems were written between 1913 and 1921 as he consolidated his values and beliefs as a Conscientious Objector. His arrest for this crime of conscience in 1917, and his subsequent prison experiences – including hunger strike – were not revealed to anyone until his deathbed. I found his diaries and his personal copies of the two books Victor Neuburg published – DAY OF LIFE and TWAIN ONE. Dad's notes within enabled me to add a date to each poem and understand better his struggle for the life he wished to live. I saw how he turned his back on his family's military history, becoming a Black Sheep. And how he fought to survive, if not thrive, in a world seemingly gone mad. His poems expressed how he felt and offered a little solace in such difficult times. He came to value the conversations and community he had with fellow inmates who shared his pacifist philosophy of life. He was a rebel, and among other rebels, he found himself.

That world was a very different place – or was it? There are still so many struggles of power, misuse of resources, violence, abuse. The struggles to become a social being believing and acting on a set of values that underpins harmony in the world. Dad didn't talk much about the richness or threadbareness of the tapestry of life. He held much of his history from me. Did I ask? Probably not! Was he trying to protect me? Probably!

I wish I had spent more time with Dad, finding out about his life and the characters whose names passed his lips during my childhood in the '50s and '60s – some of whom feature in this book, and many of whom shared his lateral, often rebellious, thinking. What he did divulge were his other passions: an international figure skating competitor, he encouraged the interest in sport and movement I hold dear to this day. I still compete in triathlons, representing the GB Age Group team, and coach and support others in maximising their performance. I remember his deep breaths and arm circling in the garden or on Hampstead Heath, and how he shared the importance of looking after our health & wellbeing, perhaps sowing the seeds for much of my career in Physical Education, Health Promotion and Professional Development.

He encouraged me to make the most of every opportunity; to be brave, try new things; to think things through and apply yourself to your principles. To travel, speak out, represent self and others to the best of your ability. And yet, despite the years he spent preaching rebellion and equality, in his own life things were different. He was judgmental and held views of femaleness and of right-and-wrong that didn't sit comfortably, but were certainly not to be challenged within his household.

He told me that I was "not very intelligent". So it was with great pride that I wore his academic gown as I collected my own Ph.D. Rebel family!

My career, unconsciously on my part, has parallel tracks to his, though nothing like the trauma that two world wars brought. The global pandemic has highlighted the huge range of philosophies and beliefs in the world that are not always synergistic and are, indeed, often adversarial.

Individuals, families, communities, countries, continents; learn together, work together, play together; listen and share.

Obsolete Spells has given context to connections that my father evolved before 1948, when he found a personal assistant who would become his wife. Dad: your dream of connection, peace and liberation lives on in those you loved. Your two daughters, Margaret and Chloe, and your four grandsons are citizens of the world.

RESOLVING DISCORDS
INTO HARMONIES

Long before I was born
A man of convictions
Found solace in poems

Thinking out of the box
The Vine Press connection
A place of sanctuary

Madness in abundance
Life was bleak and cruel
Arrest and hunger strike

Chance of a better world
Searching society
For likeminded people

Complex life tapestry
Boxes here boxes there
Family of hoarders

Galleries and dinners
Red wine in his bed springs
Paper piles on his desk

Shackled by Boarding school
Letters in envelopes
Clinging to hidden hopes

Psychology of Crime
Sex Psychotherapy
Philosophy of life

A confirmed bachelor
Eager to fall in love
Hid his inner turmoil

Discord transformation
Musical harmonies
He was living his way

Vivienne Jennings 21 October 2021

SELECTED BIBLIOGRAPHY

Books published by The Vine Press

Lillygay: An Anthology of Anonymous Poems ed. by Victor B. Neuburg. 1920.

Gabriele d'Annunzio's Appeal to Europe trans. by Hayter Preston. 1920.

Swift Wings: Songs in Sussex by Victor B. Neuburg (published anon.). 1921.

Songs of the Groves: Records of the Ancient World by Victor B. Neuburg (published anon.). 1921.

Songs of a Sussex Tramp by Rupert Croft-Cooke. 1922.

Larkspur: A Lyric Garland by and ed. by Victor B. Neuburg. 1922.

Night's Triumphs: Songs of Nature by Ernest Osgood Hanbury. 1924.

Before the Storm: Four Tales of Old Russia by The Princess Ouroussoff. 1925.

The Way of the South Wind by G.D. Martineau. 1925.

Teams of Tomorrow by G.D. Martineau. 1926.

The White Blackbird by Alfred de Musset; trans. by Henrietta Tayler. 1927.

The Story of the Sanctuary by Vera Gwendolen Pragnell. 1928.

Wot's the Game: England's Post-War Book by 'Ex-Private Billy Muggins'. 1928.

Seven Years by Shirley Tarn. 'Hermes Books No. 1'. 1928.

Day of Life by Rold White. 1929.

Twain One by Rold White. 1930.

Phantasy and Other Poems by Ethel Archer. 'Hermes Books No. 2'. 1930.

*Wax: A Drama of Evolution by Runia MacLeod. 1947.

*Chapbooks: a bibliography of references to English and American Chapbook Literature of the eighteenth and nineteenth centuries by Victor E. Neuburg. 1964.

The Way of a Virgin compiled and edited by L. and C. Brovan, printed for members of The Brovan Society, 1922. There are reasons to believe this pseudonymous collection of ostrobogulous folktales, cod-anthropology and sex-psychology essays, was made by Victor Neuburg and associates through Vine Press.

*Wax and *Chapbooks* were both published after the death of Victor B. Neuburg, but under the name, and in the spirit, of the original Vine Press.

Swift Wings and *Songs of the Groves* – as well as Neuburg's *A Green Garland* and previously unpublished *Rosa Ignota* – are available in limited facsimile editions from 100th Monkey Press via their website, www.100thmonkeypress.com.

Selected other books:

Aleister Crowley: Magick, Rock and Roll, and the Wickedest Man in the World by Gary Lachman, Tarcher, New York. 2014.

Diaries: Vol. 1 1939-1960 by Christopher Isherwood, ed. Katherine Bucknall, HarperCollins, New York. 1997.

Dylan Thomas: A New Life by Andrew Lycett, Phoenix, London. 2004.

Dylan Thomas – The Collected Letters, Volume 1: 1931-1939 ed. by Paul Ferris, W&N, London. 2017.

The Glittering Pastures by Rupert Croft-Cooke, Putnam, London. 1962.

The Great Beast – The Life of Aleister Crowley by John Symonds, Rider and Company. 1951.

The House of Vanities by Wm. Edward Hayter Preston, The Bodley Head, 1922.

Laughing Torso by Nina Hamnett, Ray Long & Richard R. Smith, New York. 1932.

The Magic of my Youth by Arthur Calder-Marshall, Rupert Hart-Davis, London, 1951.

The Magical Dilemma of Victor Neuburg by Jean Overton Fuller, First Edition, W.H. Allen, London. 1965. And Third Edition, Mandrake, Oxford. 2005. (Still in print.)

The Magical World of Aleister Crowley by Francis King, Arrow Books, 1987.

My Lord, What a Morning: An Autobiography by Marian Anderson, University of Illinois Press. 2002.

Rhythm & Colour by Richard Emerson, Golden Hare. 2018.

The Triumph of Pan by Victor B. Neuburg, introduction by Caroline Robertson, limited facsimile edition, Skoob Books, London. 1989.

Vickybird: A Memoir by his Son by Victor E. Neuburg, self-published, 1983.

Selected articles & papers:

'Full of Rich Dirt' by Arthur Calder-Marshall (review of *White Stains* by Aleister Crowley and *Magick* by John Symonds and Kenneth Grant), *TLS*, 27 July 1973.

'Lord Boleskine's Disciple' by Arthur Calder-Marshall (review of *The Magical Dilemma of Victor Neuburg* by Jean Overton Fuller), *TLS*, 13 May 1965.

'A Poet Among the Anarchists' by Caroline Robertson (Victor B. Neuburg's granddaughter), *The Raven Anarchist Quarterly* #5, Vol. 2 No. 1, Freedom Press, June 1988.

Pollen, Annebella,'"The most curious" of all "queer societies": Sexuality and Gender in British Woodcraft Camps, 1916-2016', in *Queer as Camp: Essays on Summer, Style and Sexuality*, edited by Kenneth B. Kidd and Derritt Mason. Fordham University Press, 2019.

"The Poet of Church Street" courtesy Steyning Museum. 2019.

"The Sorcerer and His Apprentice: Aleister Crowley and the Magical Exploration of Edwardian Subjectivity" by Alex Owen. *Journal of British Studies*, Vol. 36, No. 1. Jan. 1997.

"'This Shall Not Be: Behold Something Better": Seeking Sanctuary in Storrington' by Rebecca Searle. MA Dissertation, University of Sussex. 2006.

ACKNOWLEDGEMENTS

I am indebted to the efforts and generosity of the descendants of The Vine Press authors:

To Margaret Jennings-White for her beautiful afterword, and her extensive work sharing items from the archives of her father, Dr H.D. Jennings 'Rold' White. And to she and her sister, Chloe Jennings-White, and their family for sharing their family memories and White's photographs.

To Jonathan Addis, his brother Tim and their siblings for illumination on the work of their grandparents, Vera Pragnell and Dennis Earle, founders of The Sanctuary, and for the use of Dennis Earle's paintings.

To Ros Tharp and Richard Tharp for their time, candid memories and photographs of their grandmother, Runia Tharp / MacLeod. And to their cousin, Sonia Bradford, for sharing her family history and connections.

Thank you also to all the many others who made this book possible:

To Mark Pilkington, Jamie Sutcliffe and Strange Attractor Press, who make impossible things happen daily, and who believed in this project despite all available evidence. Clare Button's editorial skills and knowledge of the archive and the era were instrumental, as were Maïa Gaffney-Hyde's talents. Thanks to Richard McNeff, Richard Bancroft for their writing and reading work; to Chris Tod and Steyning Museum, Gudrun Bowers & Steyning Bookshop, Stephanie & Matthew Grant, Gluck Studio and the town of Steyning. To Paul Watson and *Rituals & Declarations* zine, in which the idea of this book was born, and to the ever-incredible Sharron Kraus. To Paul and Helen Hopper, for their lifelong encouragement and belief, and, with so much love, to Lucy and Thomas, who have been a part of this project from the very beginning.

L'ENVOY

Children, my song is sung. No more I seek
The hidden Word: my word is said, and eke
    The wheel of life hath whirled, and brought!
                                        to me
The Future in the guise of Love Antique
    That knew the songs of Grecian ecstacy.

*Of the Secret of Life and its Incommunicability. The Unknown Word
of the Stars that would be the Key of Life.*
    Life lives as Stars die; and is hence Immortal.

STRANGE ATTRACTOR PRESS
2022